I0555521

ABERRATION
SERIES
BOOK TWO

THE SHIELD

MICHEL PRINCE

THE SHIELD
Copyright © 2021 by Michel Prince

ISBN: 978-1-955784-35-1

Fire & Ice Young Adult Books
An Imprint of Melange Books, LLC
White Bear Lake, MN 55110
www.fireandiceya.com

Published in the United States of America.

Cover Design by Ashley Redbird Designs

*For those who take chances,
especially those who took a chance on me.*

CHAPTER ONE

Crawling into my closet, I laid on my back with my legs up against the wall and pulled out my journal. Light caught from my bedroom when it hit the bright pink sparkles on the cover. Desperation had me using the faux fur lined notebook purchased by my mother. As if somewhere along the way she missed when I'd turned into a dark dressing middle schooler and believed deep inside the preppy princess I'd been when I was young still existed.

At age three, I wanted a princess themed birthday. I don't remember it, that was what pictures were for, but if the frown I wore told me anything it told me I didn't want a fluffy dress and a tiara. My mother insisted I did, but I couldn't see how or why. No matter, in my mother's mind I was still three, only I went to school and not daycare. My hair was no longer ash blonde, instead I sported a chestnut coloring and even if I didn't want to admit it, parts of me were beginning to curve.

Adding to the princess persona was the prep school I attended. Uniformed, straight shot to the Ivies and a per capita trust fund population higher than the national average. The only reason I was able to stay in the exclusive private school after all our money was lost had been a mix of my grades, pitying parents and my mother's ability to screw both the wealthy and poor alike. If nothing else, my mother's inability to focus on her child had given me independence and an insatiable love of knowledge.

My scholarship, so I've been told incessantly, should be going to a better person. Someone with worth, like a savant child from an underprivileged area of town. Really, the K through twelfth school had been eyeing a kid with unbelievable times for the swim team. A grade older than me, but it wasn't as if scholarships were grade specific. Since the kid was a swimmer and not one of the bigger sports, money exceptions weren't being made. I wouldn't know about him at all if the swim coach wasn't also my English teacher.

Sad really, I used to like English. Now I wonder if he was purposely trying to tank my grades. Diagraming sentences aren't subjective like book reports and the thought of the grade I'll be receiving when I get back to school on Monday sent my stomach into a flight with butterflies in need of Ritalin.

Not only had I "embarrassed" him by calling out the error in grading, but I hadn't waited until the end of class. No, my dumb ass raised my hand, confused and actually wanting to know what I'd done wrong so I wouldn't repeat the mistake. Learning the error of my ways hadn't gone the way I'd planned. His face reddened so quick as he scanned the room and snatched my paper back to review it.

Since then I'd been moved to the back of the classroom, relegated to a row of people not interested in anything more than the latest teen magazine. Laughing at the tampon ads and trying to mimic the beauty tips given in frame by frame images on a page. Thankfully, blocking out the people around me was second nature. Most anyway. Lord knows they weren't exactly glancing my way, even if I did something that should get me noticed.

Rubbing my thumb and middle finger together, the pads of my fingers circling each other until a tingle of nerves made me have to pull them apart slowly. A blue electrical string formed as if I'd crossed a shaggy carpet in my stocking feet and reached for a doorhandle. Only there wasn't a charge. No shock, just a tingle and the further apart my finger got from my thumb, a bubble formed. Clear, the blue lightening only on the edges.

"It's okay, Ms. McArthur," my best friend's voice was unmistakable even through two doors, having me shake out my hand and bursting the bubble. "We don't need any. Oh my goodness, that's a great idea. I'll try it."

Summer Blankenship wouldn't be fooled by my empty room. Once the first door closed, the door to the closet opened.

"What's a great idea?" I asked, bending my head back and balancing on the crown.

Summer was aptly named, though currently upside down in my view she was the perky, pretty blonde with natural waves and crystalline blue eyes. Boys hung on her every word, even the high schoolers. Though I wasn't sure if that was from her perfect skin that had never known so much as a pimple or the fact she'd been in bras since last year. Today she was in a cami with an oversized sweatshirt cut around the neck so it hung off one shoulder and a pair of leggings.

"Like I listen," Summer said as she plopped next to the built-in drawers and got her phone out of her sweatshirt pouch. "Your mom gives me a new beauty tip or tells me about some show I should be watching every time I'm here. Basically, she's like the teacher on that cartoon we watch every Halloween."

"The Peanuts one?" I ask to clarify.

"Yeah, with the pumpkin kid."

"Wah, wah, wah, wah, wah, wah," I mimicked.

3

"Uh Ms. McArthur, that's so great," Summer replied with a standard response and I shook my head. "Okay, so I was totally going to call you, but this thing showed up and I had to show you."

Having a flip phone and not one of the newer ones, Summer's ability to share amazing things with me was limited. At least if you heard her tell it. I didn't mind the quiet and peace of it all, most of the time. Summer and I were rarely more than a desk apart so we could honestly share everything and usually did.

"Watch this." She showed a quick clip from an app called The Ivy. Some brother was trying to prank his sister when the girl, about our age, created a fireball and tossed it at her brother. "It's been going viral for sure. I've watched it at least a fifty times."

"Play it again," I said. "I swear these staged things pretending to be reality are so fake."

Only the girl's face went from rage to fear before the video cut off. I tapped it once more, but in the time it took to reload the video had been taken down by the company.

"They took it down," I said, passing the phone back to Summer.

"Dang it," she said, typing frantically to find it somewhere else. "I should have saved it. Ugh, I swear if my mom doesn't up my data package soon I'm going to cry."

"It wasn't real," I admonished and tucked my journal away before rolling to my side and letting my feet drop.

"Yes, it was," Summer stressed. "Very real. I told you the other day I totally stopped Stacey's cough with mind control. My mom is all about how the antibiotics in the meat are messing with kids big time."

"But you only eat organic," I countered.

"When I'm with my mom." Summer removed a binder from her wrist and pulled her hair back in a bun, her fingers tugging a bit once secured to give it the messy I didn't work hard at this look. "Something tells me your mom isn't quite as particular."

"We are nothing if not slaves to convenience. And why do the antibiotics make a difference?"

"Oh, because it weakens her immune system."

"Stacey's?" I questioned.

"Yeah, she was sick, and I cured her."

"With your mind?" My eyes narrowed, trying to catch up to my best friend's logic. Or was it a hope to be more than what we were.

"Well, I did place my hand on her back and said I hope you feel better."

"And boom, she was cured of cancer," I joked, and Summer smacked at me.

"Make fun of me all you want, but kids our age are getting powers."

"And yet, with all the provocation I get daily at school, why haven't I thrown a fireball?"

Summer had been on a kick, finding stories about superpowers. Each time she spoke of them my fingers tingled, all of them, as if triggered by the idea of others being gifted and in the back of my mind I had to wonder. I told her if she wanted to dress in a superhero cat suit with high-heeled boots do it. When she twists her ankles, I wouldn't take the blame.

"Aggie, how many more must I show you before you believe?" she asked.

"Five hundred million," I said in my best Dr. Evil voice.

"On the news they're talking about camps."

"Day camps or sleep away?" I joked, not in the mood for the conspiracy theories of Summer's mother to come spilling out. "Because that one we did at the U was pretty dang fun. Though not as educational as my mother had hoped. I think she sent me there so she could day drink."

5

"Would you be serious for one second?" she scolded.

"Deal, but you have to admit that at some point the blogs your mother gets her info from aren't exactly scholarly."

Summer narrowed her eyes at me. Why would she want powers? Or to stand out? At this point, she was already near the top of the social structure at school. Or would be if she dropped me as a friend. Then again, if she brought up the insane theories around most in our class, they would make her a tinfoil hat and call it a day. We would both be banished to a table by the column instead of the corner table where you could survey all the glory that was the cafeteria. I'm surprised a throne hadn't been erected for those few, like Summer, to fight over. I was the jester at the end of the table, forced to keep my back to the rest of the undesirables.

Or was I in the first row of loyal disciples? The simple rules of elementary school had morphed from don't be the kid with tuna fish in your lunch box, to a uniform is the base layer of your outfit. One must accessorize and wear the correct shoes. Socks were our rebellion. Customizable and getting to be expensive. The last thing you wanted to be was the girl wearing the uniform pants instead of the skirt.

"What if the vaccines we received as babies are finally kicking in and mutating our genes?"

There was an awkward silence. Her mother had been an early anti-vaxxer, convinced Summer would get autism, stroke out at six-months or die. It took her father, three doctors and a group of lawyers to force the issue when her parents were divorcing. Basically, if her mother wanted to have primary custody, child support and a bonus when it came to alimony, she would have to get Summer up to date on her vaccinations. When it came down to it, the fear for her child's wellbeing was outweighed by her mother's desire for a payday.

Sadly, none of this we should have ever known, much like the crap my mother pulled. Yet sheltering us from an unproven side effect was somehow more important than very adult issues. The grown-up issues came front and center during open discussion. Speak to your child as an adult and they will be one was a theory embraced by both our mothers.

"While I do love your closet, any reason why we're in here?" Summer picked up a pair of ballet flats in like new condition and inspected them.

My walk-in-closet was more than I deserved really. The six by eight space was the same size as my father's prison cell. No matter how tight Summer and I were, I could never tell her it was the only time I felt close to the man. My mother would never take me to see him. Having moved on with her life, the last thing she wanted was a reminder of money owed to all he'd swindled. Even now she was looking into changing not only her last name, but mine too.

No matter what my father did to others, the only hurt I experienced was him not being there for me. Most days, he'd been willing to drop anything for me. More than my mother had been, and for some reason. Even now I wondered if she would rather be done with me, too.

"I'd say noise proofing," I replied, standing, stretching and pushing aside a few dresses more to knock off dust than actually make a fashion choice. "But there's a vent in here for some strange reason."

"Oh, have you been spying on your mother?"

"God no, the last thing I want to know is what she's doing."

When I was younger, in the big house with a pool, maintenance men came by and what did I know about the schedule for grown-up things? All I knew were the men smirked at me in a way that made me uncomfortable. Like they knew something about me or my family, I didn't. I've never been one for smirkers in general.

The doorbell rang, the sound echoing through the vent,

followed by footsteps. I tugged on Summer's outstretched hand to help her up when the voice of her own mother made her stop at the doorway.

"They're upstairs," my mother said. "Who are those men outside?"

Of course, my mother noticed men. She probably was going into scan and assess mode. I crossed to my window to see a dark suburban with men spaced out from next to the rear passenger door and along our lawn and driveway. They were wearing windbreakers with yellow writing on the front and back. But a mix of distance, angles and their body position made it hard to determine who they worked for.

"Did your mom get bodyguards?" I questioned and turned back to see Summer's face had paled. The normally sun kissed skin shouldn't have that ability and yet, here she was one shade above pure white as fear had my best friend trembling. "What is it?"

"They're here for me."

Four years later.

Strange how normal the abnormal can become. There was a time when I couldn't take a long car ride without breaks, let alone read while doing it. The motion too much for me. Maybe not having a window was saving me from needing to puke and hide under the covers. Now when the train stops, the solid, firm ground makes me feel uneasy. Like returning to Earth after floating in space and we had only been on the rails for a week.

When Riley Weston and Trent Marcus joined forces and suggested we take the railcars we were living in down and turn Satori, our camp, into a mobile unit, we were all skeptical.

Maybe it was the nearness to almost dying that had me uneasy and not the idea of constantly being in motion. Our once vast suites were now split off into four units with one long wall to create a hallway.

The rooms were closer to normal sized bedrooms now, and I was no longer in a single suite, not because I was a *Harvey*, but because everyone had to share. *Harveys,* or as they older *aberrations* called them *unblessed*, were those whose powers either had yet to emerge or lacked them all together. While Summer had kept me up on all we had learned over the years since *aberrations* began plaguing the world, it was nothing compared to living in Satori. The crash course in class warfare and the general way the world sucks when you're different.

"It's like we're in a lockdown camp without being in a lockdown camp," Breonna, my roommate, said after tossing a book to the side. Her natural curls were creating a dark halo effect with one unruly one falling over her deep ash colored eye. Stunning, with no make-up, the girl's doe eyes and flawless, burnt umber, colored skin practically glowed.

Breonna had met me a few times when I was classified as a *Harvey.* The first few days of laundry duty I'd been working intake. Making sure people's drop offs and pick-ups were done properly. It helped me learn about the exchange rate we used and proved what I thought I had down when I arrived was far from accurate. But since my bestie, and only person I knew beyond Riley, was shacking up with her boyfriend, both Breonna and I were paired off in some random drawing of names. Part of me wondered if that was how colleges did it, not that college would ever be in my future. At least not in the foreseeable future. Then again, I hadn't been in school for over two years now and catching up wasn't exactly my first go to if I ever got out in regular society again.

"It's not so bad," I replied, though boredom was sinking in and there had to be something I could do to pass the time.

Maybe I should sweet talk Riley into pulling me a board game next time I saw him. If I ever saw him again. Old high and mighty vice president doesn't randomly drop in my room anymore. No longer my neighbor or with the ease of stepping between cars.

"Aggs, you don't get it, there was this totally sweet show on the Nigerian channel that was just getting good."

Aggs, short for Aggie, short for Agatha, had been co-opted by all on the rolling safe space. Another of the abnormal becoming normal in my life. Being hated, I'd gotten used to years ago when my father was arrested but hunted. That was only a few years old. Yet all of us determined to be dangerous based on our birthdate now suffered it. A whole year's worth of children written off and marked by the randomness of our conception.

Breonna was a *translator*, but not like she'd spent years learning other languages or was even brought up in an ESL, English as a second language home. Nope, she was blessed. One who earned the whole *aberration* status by having a power. She could understand and talk to anyone. Not in some sweet as therapy way. Nope, she literally could understand every language from every man, woman or beast, as they say. Bring a dog in crying in pain and you'll get a broken story about what happened. According to Breonna, while animals had a language, it didn't track like humans did. Similar to sign language, there was a shorthand a hearing person would see as missing words. Or when I took that German class back in junior high and we learned their nouns and verbs weren't in the same order as English speakers.

What would have happened to her if she'd gone to a camp? The government ones wanted skills that could be used in war. No matter what they told the parents, who, through duty or fear, had handed over their child to them. The United States wasn't alone in the practice. We weren't some shining paragon of virtue. You could see it in the eyes of generals and colonels, explaining what was happening there. Strange that my mother actually protected me while Summer's mother had shipped her off at the first offer placed. Believing the lies without any hesitation about fostering the gifts and helping the children develop. As if we had agility with a ball or an aptitude to music that only needed a little assistance to guide us to some future career.

"I need a massive screen," Breonna moaned as she sat up on the side of her bed and held her phone in the air, her eyes cutting to the TV still on the floor because mounting it wasn't taking priority at the moment. "With streaming stations ready to be flipped. Seriously, how can you stand watching a handful of Blu-rays over and over again?"

I wasn't at the moment watching any movies. For me, they were a way to drown out the noise and fall asleep. There was a study done on people watching the same thing over and over again. The comfort, much like reading the same book again and again. You know the ending, maybe you'll see something new, but for the most part the anxious parts aren't going to cause stress and no matter what I put out to the world, I was a ball of stress inside. That is why I usually went to sleep watching one of the Lord of the Ring trilogy movies. They were old and soothing.

"You want me to check and see if anyone wants to swap? I heard Gordon is into cult classics," I offer.

"Any chance you know how long we'll be circling the country like hobos?" she asked the question all of us were wondering about. This incognito way of travel was a band-aide to a very large bullet wound I'd seen first-hand and relived in vivid nightmares.

"The rest of our life? Or until President Marcus gets kicked out of government," I reasoned. There was no immediate plan to stop, but the election was less than two weeks away and polls weren't favoring the incumbent.

While our group of hidden dangers had the plus of hiding the President's son, it only bought us time and a little extra protection. Once he was out of office, we would be out of luck. Sadly, that wasn't the current priority of those in charge. No, that was currently held by a *leaper* named Taylor we needed to rescue. Kidnapped by her psycho boyfriend in some cultish ritual to kill Riley, it appeared. All of it, once again becoming normal.

Slipping from my bed, I finally became cognizant of the movement. Vibration underneath my feet, knocking me off balance and causing Breonna to look at me as if I were crazy. The train wasn't going at some breakneck speed or around a curve. Last I heard, we were in Montana taking our time and would be stopping at some point to allow work to be done on the train and because who, beyond cows and sheep, were out at night in Montana. For the most part, we've been staying west of the Mississippi River because of the sparse population allowing us all sorts of room to roam.

"You good, Aggs?" Breonna asked, though she hadn't moved so much as her eyes from her phone screen.

"Fine, just thinking about wandering up and down the hall."

Our freight cars currently didn't have the connecting compartments, which meant when in motion I could only go so far. Hopefully, we'd figure out a way to fix this because the bathrooms were four cars in either direction for me. A stopping point luxury that needed to be remedied sooner rather than later.

Stepping out into the hall, I found I wasn't alone. One of my neighbors was out and running laps, it seemed. Headphones in, all I got was an irritated glare barely visible in the dim light of the makeshift home we now all occupied.

Only a week into this whole cluster of crap, I'd yet to meet all twelve of my fellow riders. With two *Harvey* pods and two *aberration* pods, there was a bit of tension among those who had and who didn't. Then again, if four people, instead of two, were jammed into my pod I'd be upset too.

"Sadie," the girl said as she tapped the wall, turned and headed to the other end of the freight car, her purple streaked hair swishing back and forth in her ponytail.

"Aggie, Aggs, really."

"I know," she replied, her breathing even considering she was jogging.

"I thought Dina was our only *reader*?" I questioned.

Sadie slowed down and finally stopped. Scooping up a water bottle with a dozen brightly colored stickers on it from the floor outside what I assumed was her door. A middle door. A *Harvey* door.

"You don't need to be a *reader* to know what people are thinking, Aggie." Sadie let out a long breath, then took a drink.

"I suppose not. You're brave, drinking when we don't know where our next stop is."

"Should be in a half hour, max." Sadie leaned her back on the wall. "So, Aggs what are you?"

"A *shield* maybe."

"Maybe?" Sadie snorted, her features a strange mix of ethnicity. The more I took her in, the more confused I was by her. "Newly found or newly claimed?"

"Found," I said, straightening my shoulders a bit. Claimed was a nasty way of saying someone was faking their power.

Powers, newer ones at least, were hard to harness and a person could say they had experienced an ability. Lord knows Riley could barely tap into *pushing* when he arrived and now, he was the *amalgam*. A mix of all powers coming to him in harsh bursts obtained when correctly touched by another

13

aberration. His ability to absorb powers had us all questioning his sanity for a few months. The secret he kept from me, of all people.

Tall and athletic, I wondered if Sadie was part of the security detail. They would know our stopping spots. Eyeing the maturity of her face, I became a bit uneasy, wondering why we didn't all step out when in motion to meet each other. It was as if we're all locked away in cells instead of a community of misfits trying to conform. Maybe she was closer to seventeen. Were January babies our elders in a way?

"I came here as a *Harvey*," I confessed, hoping to build a bridge.

Normally I'm closed off. Wary of people, but Riley and Taylor, both taught me to take chances. We're all locked in until a better solution was found and I'd need to expand my circle. Then again, I'd doubled it by allowing Riley in, and that should have been commended. The baby steps I was taking, the last thing I wanted to do was leap head-first into an ocean. It was better to have ten loyal friends, then ten thousand followers.

"I'm not a *Harvey*," she replied, dropping the water bottle to hold it by the hook on the top and the stickers were on full display. Rainbows, a Cal-State sticker, and an Army one. "Contiguous."

"Older, I assume," I said, the term for those punished for being born close to the year two-thousand.

"Ninety-eight, I was all ready to sign up to be all I could be at Cal-State's ROTC when the laws got extended, by the time they were rescinded my drive to follow in my daddy's footsteps and join anything run by the government had faded."

"I'm sure he understood," I reasoned, rocking back on my heels a bit unsure what to do with a person now hired on to be our helpers, the protectors that could get us food and transport us without question. Four digits on their license saving them from our fate. One, I've recently learned, will not end any time in the near future.

"There are many ways I've disappointed him since then. Not jumping back in and going to college being step one."

The train was beginning to slow, the vibration under my booted feet sending signals of impending freedom.

"I have to get my shower stuff before my shift," Sadie said, wiping her brow. "Nice to meet someone beyond my roomies, Aggie."

"Guess I can't help but see you around," I replied, thinking one at a time I can let people in as the air rushed from my lungs. Sucked out as if a vacuum was pulling all the oxygen from the bags and a ghost-like figure was running from me. Had my soul been snatched? My arms stretched out as I fell forward with only the image of Riley, the floppy haired boy who'd been my neighbor, with a face full of panic staring back at me.

CHAPTER TWO

"Whoa, Aggs, I'm so sorry." Riley's apology was falling on my very confused ears. Wasn't he three cars away from me? The practically royal suite of the administration around here.

"Riley, what the heck?"

"Wow, that was weird, I've never gone through someone before." The boy was still lost in himself and some newly found power. Repeatedly flipping his hands over as if there were somehow going to fall off.

"How did you get—did you just say you went through me?" I barked, my hands covering my chest as if it had been violated in some strange way.

"Okay, hear me out, so, there's a *vapor* in Satori now." His bright eyes were lit up from excitement more than the dim lights we kept in the hallway. The freckles peppering his nose were less prevalent than before. Even the baby face had lost the bit of roundness it'd once possessed.

"A *vapor*?" I questioned because with each new power came a new name to describe it and while I'd just seen Riley as a ghost, *vapor* wasn't my first thought.

"Yeah, turning me into a gas, gasses can make it through

porous places." His glee wasn't calming me in any way, shape, or form.

"The railcar is steel."

"Micro-fissures can happen," he explained as my mind swirled with the newly found knowledge. His excitement had his eyes wide, and I wondered where the petrified kid I'd met a few months ago had disappeared to. Through a micro-fissure, it appears. "Like air pockets, enough I can squeeze through."

"Then why aren't you a stream instead of the whole you? I think ghoster would be a better name."

"But *vapor* sounds more ominous." His eyes were a mix of smiling and dark.

"Like a DC character, got it, well, I'm going to need a shower and please, for the love of all that is holy, tell me you didn't leave any of your bits inside of me."

Riley's eyes widened even further. "I don't know. I've never gone through anyone before."

"How does that work again? Because I don't have holes, unless you count my earring holes."

"Please, you're about as porous as they come."

"Are you saying I'm basically a sea cucumber?" I asked, trying to think of anything I'd heard was little more than a processing plant for liquid.

"No—of course not—it's just skin, you know—"

His face was flushing red. Sadly for him, my enjoyment over seeing him squirm was worth more to me than letting him off the hook. Below me the train was slowing, and I hadn't prepared for the jerking stop that flung me into his very corporeal arms. Reminding me how much I missed the slight touches we'd shared in the past. The warmth of his palm to my arm, even when I had a light sweatshirt on there was still a connection. I didn't want to admit it had always been there. Even now when he isn't the petrified cute boy sitting next to me on a beat-up couch in the back of a U-Haul. My life had prepared me to be hardened on the outside. Fake it until you make it. Sadly, the McArthur family mantra had landed my father in jail and drained our assets. Riley, on the other hand, was of the hide and hope the danger passes clan.

"I saved your life," he joked, brushing back my loose hair. "Guess I'm forgiven."

"Guess again, brat," I said, pushing him away. "My shield didn't pop up so obviously I sensed no danger."

The damn superpower I possessed was as reliable and tamed as a feral cat. Sure, it might show up if someone leaves out a saucer of milk, but don't expect it to come with a simple here kitty, kitty. Nope, it was on its own schedule and even with a month or so called "training" I had as much control of it as I did my knee when tapped on the tendon. Reflex was the best I could muster and that hadn't stopped a blade from slicing open Riley's mother when the shield was set to protect me. Pushing her into the blade with only Summer's healing abilities saving the woman.

"You saying I didn't even scare you a tiny bit?" he asked.

"You choked me a bit," I admitted. "What can I say? I breathe oxygen, not Riley vapors, the mixture of seventy thousand powers mixed with insecurity, doubt and questioning levels of ability."

"Ouch." His face fell and regret instantly eked along my spine.

It was a cheap shot coming from a place I didn't enjoy, but I'd let the guy into my inner circle…and strangely through my body. Currently, I was not only slightly violated but also hurt from a severe lack of attention. Summer was the one who did the boyfriend thing, not me, and that made the fact I was not only having feelings but allowing them to make me act a certain way beyond irritating. I was the ice queen. The unfeeling girl who kissed Riley in public and his first response was to tell me people could see me expressing an emotion and I didn't care. All of these facts swam around in my head, heart and other places, confusing me more because his first thought wasn't to kiss me back. No, his sweetheart of softy parts wanted to make sure I was okay first. Jerk.

"What's on tonight's agenda?" I asked since when we stopped everyone would be buzzing around like bees trying to finish off projects to make this temporary situation livable.

"You didn't get your orders?"

"I have orders now," I countered. I may have been better off when I was a *Harvey* with a schedule of menial tasks allowing me access to food.

"Peyton did give you a phone, right?" Riley questioned as the doors to the suites opened and my neighbors made their way to the end of the railcar to get out. Their eyes confused by the male in our midst.

Riley's hand gently brushed on my upper arm to move me out of the way of the exiting girls. My skin rose and belly tightened. *Never look away when confronting Agatha*, unlike Riley, I knew when my father spoke it was all a memory. I could pinpoint the day, time and place if I thought hard enough. Only this wasn't a confrontation, this was a touch. Simple, sweet, protective from a guy I know likes me for who I am. At least on one level.

Pulling in on my lips didn't help because I'd lost the bit of moisture in my mouth. Riley gave me a sweet smile and quirked his head to the side. He wanted something from me. Fluttering in my belly sent heat searing to my face.

"Did he?"

"Did who what?"

"Peyton," he said, his fingers curling around mine in a playful way. "Give you a phone?"

"Oh, right, that—"

"There you are." Dina's head popped in the doorway at the

19

end of the railcar and Riley's fingers disappeared from mine, causing my heart to clench.

Dina's jet-black hair with streaks of electric blue were fashioned into the milkmaid braids today. Layered long sleeves with a *Thresher* T-shirt on top wasn't enough to keep her warm, if the rubbing of her arms was any indication. And while Riley liked me, Dina was pretty high on his list of important people, too. We both tended to rock kicker boots. She tended to define her almond-shaped eyes with thick liner, while I rocked the just rolled out of bed and not in the fake social media perfect face lie.

"Trent sent a group text," Dina explained, with her fingers wiggling. "Looking for you and Petra to start doing the whole *laser* thing."

"Right, I better go," Riley said, stepping to the side. The back of his hand brushed against mine, but I couldn't tell if it was an accident or on purpose. A way of saying goodbye privately to me and, worse yet, I wanted to know the answer. "Sorry, Aggs, about the whole—"

"Floating through me, yeah, I'm gonna need therapy and to find an adult beverage at some point." Turning my head down, I kept my back to Dina and hoped my voice hadn't cracked when I replied. A girl needs to keep her hard as nails don't give a flying hockey puck about anything persona.

"I'll check with my mom later about the whole leaving bits." Riley disappeared, and I headed back into my suite to gather stuff for a shower. Digging out a coat since we had found winter if the white flakes that drifted in were any indication.

"Lucky," Dina said, and I jumped a bit in surprise that she'd waited outside my suite.

"How's that?" I questioned, worried she was thinking about my nearness to Riley as a plus. Not normally one to want something it was strange I had become a bit possessive of

Riley as of late. "He's learning a new power and popped in here."

"Huh?" Dina's head quirked to the side and her eyes narrowed a bit.

Had Riley visited her suite with his new power? Maybe he'd been past her, and she understood he was wandering, which meant nothing special about being around me. It was an accident.

"I was talking about the fact you get a shower this break. That and you have a winter coat."

"Oh." My face burned from embarrassment. "Minnesota girl, kinda standard operating gear."

Sure, Riley and I had kissed and, from what I'd heard, Dina probably passed her power to him through a similar method. Even when we had a moment, it wasn't some big deal. It turned out because when we returned to Satori his focus was on saving Taylor and not setting up any type of ground rules or clarification around him, me and Dina. Both of us were probably in the same head space about him. At least I hoped we were, and I wasn't some lovesick fool unaware of the situation.

"But I can't say I was surprised when I saw him in here. The place was quiet, and that's why I looked."

The explanation one most in the world didn't understand. Even if the world accepted *aberrations* had powers, they didn't understand the limitations and the burdens of them. Being a *reader* meant Dina could hear thoughts. All the time. Without wanting to or probing. The constant chatter enough to drive anyone insane and from the description not even noise cancelling headphones on blast could totally mute them.

Only if a person had the ability to block, or in my case shield themselves from the invasion of privacy. Ironic that would be my gift. Maybe that was how they were chosen. Riley accepted everyone on face value, and he was the

21

amalgam. The one *aberration* who has the ability to accept all the gifts from everyone. Learn new powers and wield them as needed. I, on the other hand, blocked people and kept them at a distance.

Then why was Dina a *reader*? For her, it was a curse, having to hear everyone all the time. Maybe retribution for her being a gossip in kindergarten? Or she knew more than she should about people just by looking at them.

"Weren't you supposed to be doing protection duty?" Dina asked as she fingered my towel.

"Must have missed the text," I lied, taking a step back to give myself a bit of personal space. I had checked the phone when I was gathering my items and I was supposed to sit sentry. Obviously, Peyton hadn't checked the shower rotation because I was on that schedule too. "Besides, we have *cloakers.* Is it really snowing because it's Montana in late October or is the *forecaster* doing their thing?"

"I'm thinking Montana, but—" Dina popped her head out of the door for a moment before coughing and pressing her back against the metal wall. "That wind is no joke. Jesus take the wheel. If our *forecaster* is doing that, I'm going to throttle them."

Zipping up, I tugged down my beanie and stepped out. The first step had the snow ankle deep with a hard crunch. Any air I had was practically sucked from my lungs for a moment as wind blasted past me with thick, fluffy snow turning into icy daggers. Being from Minneapolis proper, I could handle snow, even cold, but as they always say it's not the air temperature, it was the wind chill. Turning the particles into a blanket of frost; slamming into you like a skidding semi. Breathing out my body became encased in my shield, and I was unsure if it was the snow, cold or the fact I couldn't refill my lungs, causing it to appear. A sound, similar to a woodpecker ticking from every direction alerted me to its presence even before the ease of the wind. The weather had turned violent, but with my crystal shield, it simply swooshed around me as if I were a railcar.

Trudging through the thick snow, I made my way five cars down to the one set up as a shower car for the girls.

Only two cars were equipped for showers with a schedule stricter than before until we could get cars linked. Four cars were for basic bathroom needs, co-ed in that case because it would be too hard to separate at this point. All of it a mess and I didn't care if I was supposed to be a shield and watching out for dangers. The snow could handle that duty for me for at least a few minutes. It wasn't like I could do anything but get petrified and create a bubble about the size of me. No matter how much Peyton our *seer* believed it was my destiny, visions were ideas, not facts set in stone. There was no guarantee behind his words, and that was why he made them convoluted. Allowing a wide swath of options like a horoscope, and I was but one. I hadn't gotten to shower since before my suite went mobile and the last thing I wanted to do was skip it on the off chance I could save just myself while on sentry duty.

A cry of mutual complaint went out when I opened the end of the car where a makeshift sliding door had been installed. Steam escaped the space as a *Harvey* with power issues glared at me.

"You were supposed to knock," she growled.

"You're supposed to be outside the door," I countered in a way I was a bit ashamed of since I'd been in the faux power position before and was talked down to by more than one *aberration* in my tenure of laundry duty.

Having been a *Harvey* when I arrived, due to my lack of disclosure and the fact I wasn't actually sure my electric finger bubbles were an actual power, I was a second-class citizen. Cursed to be born in the year two-thousand without powers, but still condemned. For that reason, I knew this girl's pain. Stuck in the showering area like a hallway monitor, just to earn a few food credits granted to the *aberration* by their ability to do something special.

"What's your name?" she asked, snagging a clipboard from the wall.

"Aggie, Agatha McArthur," I said as the girl scanned the lines.

"You're early, two minutes and stall six should be open." With a hard check of her pen, the girl hung the board up on the wall again. "Don't turn off the water, just step out. We do as quick of a swap as we can, or we'll lose the heat from the spray."

"So, I am supposed to stand naked outside the sixth stall?"

"If you want to get in on time, yes, but you can have a towel wrapped around you. There's a hook."

If only my shield wasn't invisible. A knock sounded and the gatekeeper gave me a hard glare. Guess some people got the memo I missed. Uncomfortably, I began stripping down and placed my clothes in a plastic tub opposite the stalls. Tucking the towel tight around my chest and wondering if that would have been the way it would have happened if I'd have made it to a high school gym class. Even in middle school, we hadn't been forced to change our clothes for gym class.

Shaking off the thoughts of normalcy, my toes curled on the wet floor covered in foam mats, probably pulled from a kids catalog because they reminded me of ones from a preschool playroom. Slipping on my slides, I pushed forward to make sure there was enough grip. I only wore them in the shower since they were communal, but they were already getting pretty beaten up. In front of me, a line of stalls with a shower curtain hung and a hook was placed just outside each one. There was a large digital clock above each of the stalls so the person showering and the person waiting could see the countdown.

The wall behind me was metal shelving with various tubs, thankfully large enough to accommodate coats. Even with the steam standing in just a towel watching others arrive, each opening of the door sucking the heat from the space, made me wonder if I stood outside the door could I protect the opening and allow others through with my shield. A loud beeping jarred me from my thoughts, followed by a groan from stall six as a hand reached from behind the curtain to grab a towel.

Steadying myself to do the swap. Summer moved the curtain to the side with the towel around her body and her long blonde hair twisted to the side in a thick, wet clump. Natural curl was in stark contrast to the stick straight stuff I sported. Even with the best perm in the world, I couldn't get so much as a wave.

"Well, if I'd have known you were waiting behind me, I would have just waved you in." Summer beamed.

"Haven't we moved past bath time buddies," I teased as I stepped by the curtain with my toiletries and hung my towel on the hook just outside the closed curtain.

"Yeah, but thirty whole minutes in a shower might be worth doubling up," Summer spoke loud enough to be heard over the water.

Sadly, the spray wasn't scalding hot the way I preferred, but at this point jumping into a cold waterfall would be a blessing. When I was younger and in mandatory therapy, mandatory in the fact my mother had to show the damage caused by my father, the shrink used to ask me about my room. Was it clean or dirty? Had I showered, brushed my teeth or changed my clothes? As far as I could tell, I didn't have some rank B.O. making the woman ask questions. Instead, I soon learned the simple act of showering each day could stave off depression, and at this point in my life I needed every possible way to fight off the looming, dark, clouded bitch.

The act of caring enough for oneself could have a greater effect on a person than eating healthy or working out. Though the woman suggested the three things as some sort of natural serotonin boosting triple cocktail. My mother chose a different triple cocktail involving a daily dose, mixed with an emergency dose when life got really hard, both washed down with wine, a shot or something poured over ice as if I couldn't smell the liquor and actually believed it was tea.

At least for me, the showering stuck. Even the quick five-minute ones they got to take when the camp wasn't mobile had helped. Taking me away from the reality of being hunted with little to no place where I could hide,

"Where is your suite now?" Summer asked. "I feel all trapped not being able to just walk around. This train better find a home soon."

"Don't think that's going to happen," I said, then thought better of her answer. Summer was the girlfriend to the man in charge. The president in a way of Satori. As first lady, maybe she knew things I didn't.

"A girl can dream, can't she? How's your new roommate? Does it suck having one? You'd think we could text more at least, but noooooo, Peyton's all *we have to be really careful now*."

This form of twenty thousand questions was Summer's baseline. It was best to let her get them all out before even trying to answer. My only issue was taking in the barrage of questions as I tried to wash my hair. The giant digital display might as well be a ticking clock with how loud it seemed with each second going backwards on the display. Or maybe that was all in my mind.

A crash of cold tore through the barriers and I understood the screams from before as a howl unconsciously burst from deep inside me. The water temperature meeting the outside air in some sick, twisted "let's make snow inside" type of way. I was scared to reach out and brace myself for fear of my skin fusing to any exposed metal. Without thought, the water no longer touched my skin, and I glanced up to see a bubble around me. The best way of seeing my shield for the first time. Even with the snow, I couldn't make out the boundaries. Water, still a bit icy, cascading over the safety of my shield as I watched it rush along the sides gave a perfect outline.

Beautiful in a way, the streaks not unfamiliar, they reminded me of the big clear umbrella I had as a kid. The domed top keeping me from freezing. The water crystalized for a moment, then returned to liquid, and I knew the moment had passed. Letting my guard down enough as I watched the shield shift up from my feet like a glass cake topper being removed. Above me, a bright red digital display warned me I had less than five minutes left before I'd need to go.

"Um, Aggs," Summer said from the other side of the curtain.

"Yes," I replied, my focus on the quick scrubbing of my hair as shampoo rinsed down my back, causing bubbles to pool at my feet.

"Why did the curtain puff out like a fat lady in a Mumu?"

"Your gift is offensive, mine is defensive," I explained. "And as much as I'd like to say I have control at this point, anything that is potentially harmful makes it come out."

"Oh my god, you're like a boy now." Her laugh and comment made me pull the curtain enough to pop my head out and glare at her.

"In what possible way am I a guy?"

"Think about it," she challenged and wiggled her eyebrows. "Just replace pain with a pretty girl, Ryan Reynolds shirtless for others or heck a stiff breeze that tickles them just right."

"I need to condition." I snapped the curtain closed and

checked the time. That's it. I will be paying the premium for two in one shampoo next time I get supplies. There isn't enough time to shampoo, condition and scrub myself. Flat hair it is, good thing that was my standard look anyway.

"Wait, could we walk outside in your shield in bikinis and not be cold?" Summer questioned.

"Darn it, I left my bikini in my other super, secret hide away camp," I snarked. "Guess we won't find out today."

"Well, that was poor planning on your part."

The bell rang above me, and I reached for my towel to wrap around my chest and try to not get in the spray. An irritated girl stood in line as if Summer combing the snarls from her wet hair by the shower was a major issue. Both she and I moved past Summer and once I could set down my plastic basket of toiletries, I twisted my hair to squeeze out the extra water.

The room was filling up as more people were coming for their assigned times, while others were trying to dry off and get dressed. Sadie had a hairdryer and others were showing their jealousy as they tousled their hair with damp towels. Summer, of course, waltzed up to her and tapped her shoulder. Some trade negotiations were being had that seemed to involve me if the pointing of my bestie was any indication. I wonder if this was how it was done before the invention of currency. Ms. Weston would know, the woman was a few millennium old. Less than a minute later, Summer was waving me over and I pulled my hoodie over my head, finally releasing my towel to be transferred to my hair.

"What's up?" I asked, rubbing my towel to my wet hair.

"Sadie here says she knows you," Summer said. "And that you two are neighbors."

"Yeah, we just met," I replied, thinking a few minutes of conversation hadn't garnered me any special treatment.

"Perfect, then you can bring her dryer back to your suite

for safe keeping." Summer brought her hands together. "Who says fate doesn't exist?"

"Fate? Really?" I scoffed, because fate wasn't exactly my friend.

"Think about it. You and Sadie were on the same schedule for a shower as me," Summer said. "And both of you love me dearly."

"Uh huh." I replied because most people that met Summer loved her dearly. Running into more than one in the shower wasn't exactly Serendipity.

Sadie passed the hairdryer to Summer who smiled in triumph. "I wouldn't be alive if it weren't for Summer and her healing touch."

"She does have mad *save the human type skills*," I replied. I'd seen more than experienced her bringing people from the brink of death. All of it more than I wanted to remember at the moment. I'll save those visions for my nightmares where they belonged. At least I stopped waking up screaming and covered in sweat before I was put into a shared space with Breonna.

"Well, I gotta go play train engineer for a few hours," Sadie said, gathering her bag and slinging it over her shoulder.

If she said any more, I hadn't heard it. The jet plane engine noise from the blowing hair dryer was blocking out sounds. If only they could block out the longing looks we were receiving from the other girls coming out of the cue.

With dry hair and bundled up in our coats, we made our way out of the shower railcar, and I finally took in what I could see of the area. Wind whipped snow around, creating swirls, and I realized the snow had stopped falling. Only the wind remained and if I focused hard enough, maybe I could conjure my bubble wide enough for both Summer and me. Then again, it wasn't like I yelled out shield and it appeared.

Summer linked her arm through mine as we both tried to

balance. Now I was the one getting flashbacks of us in the wintertime at recess. Skipping our way arm in arm to the spot where the snowplow had pushed all the snow to. A giant pile we and the other kids had been working on for at least a week to carve out a cave in the back. Snow whipped against my face like fairy daggers, stinging my eyes, and my shield appeared. Summer snuggled closer to me, her head resting on my shoulder. Inside my protective bubble, the howling was muted. Others were moving around. A mix of bathroom, food and just needing space runs. A snowball fight was being waged between the railcars and in the distance, I could see sparks flying from red-hot embers.

Petra and Riley must be working on the necessary welding if we were going to link the railcars together a bit. Sectioned out of course, but all amazing to me. We hadn't finished high school. Some never made it to eighth grade graduation before being snatched and sent off or going into hiding. Yet here we were with only a handful of adults helping us create a whole new world. The sprinkling of hope on the horizon enough to keep me stepping forward in life.

CHAPTER THREE

"Okay, that was so cool," Summer said once we got back to my suite. "It was like an inside out snow globe."

"It kinda was," I admitted, still unsure if it was me projecting my shield or if it was the reaction to the cold. Having extended my shield to Summer made me feel like I'd accomplished something, no matter how minor.

Flopping on my bed, I reached for a pillow and hugged it close to me. Summer sat next to me, and I was happy to still be able to have a decent sized bed. When they were sectioning off pods, I wasn't sure, but Breonna and I were able to make it work. Our place would give a person with OCD twitches. The beds not lined up because by placing them slightly off it allowed them to fit. Hers was pressed into the far corner. While mine was far enough from the door you could open it, but against the shared wall with the *Harveys* next door.

Breonna had her clothes and belongings in three different chests, while I had a dresser across from my bed. TV on the floor, a mix of fantasy pictures and anime were hand painted, drawn, or sketched on the wall. In another life Breonna would have travelled the world capturing its beauty in multicolored charcoals. My favorite feature along my wall were the bolts. Used to secure the bunk beds in the next pod served as hooks for me and I tossed by towel on one to let it air dry. Others were giving me a way to keep my cords from tangling.

My phone buzzed at the edge of my bed, the text message lighted up the screen and telling me it wasn't alone. There were others, probably with similar, but less demanding requests. All of which had me sighing.

We have a new person that needs escorting. Get to the front of the train now.

"Does Trent not understand I have zero control over my shield?" I questioned Summer whose head was tilted to the side and eyes focused on one of Breonna's darker sketches. "Hello, Summer."

"Huh?" she shook her head, clearing her thoughts. "What happened?"

"I'm supposed to be a bodyguard? Has Trent seen me? I'm five foot nothing, with the ninja skills of a drunk squirrel."

"Oh my God, did you see that video with the squirrel that ate a fermented pumpkin?" Summer laughed, and I needed her to focus beyond the fuzzy, nut hoarding, rodent with a bushy tail. "It couldn't even stand upright. They said it was fine, but who knew that was even a thing?"

"Back to my question? Does he think I'm a tour guide or am I actually supposed to provide some sort of protection?"

Summer tilted her head to see my phone and shrugged. "I think that's Riley's aunt. Gil was doing a retrieval and meeting us out here."

"The one Vince tortured?" I asked, the whole history one I couldn't even imagine surviving.

"Yep, Vince's mother, if you can believe that. She was gathering things for us, and I guess Ms. Weston had to convince her to come."

Summer's phone buzzed, and she groaned. "Someone

32

broke their leg in the shower, at least it better be that or I'll do it for him. I can't wait until Riley's not being used for all the stupid train things and can take this crap."

"Bundle up," I said, "You're going solo this time."

"I'm going to find Riley and Petra and make them get our cars connected ASAP." Summer gave me a tight hug. "I miss your face Aggs."

Sending a quick text back to let them know I was on my way as I bundled up, too. The small mirror we'd placed on the back of our door caught me off guard. My hazel green eyes stopping me. I rarely looked at myself. Selfies had never been my thing and most days the last thing I cared about was how I appeared. Although my ears were pierced, I never wore anything more than two small hoops and a few studs. Pulling my hair into two ponies at the base of my neck, I tugged on a skull cap and headed out. Glad I was only twenty cars from the front, making it easier for me to see the front verses the back. Lord knows I would have been pissed if I would have gone in the wrong direction. A regular old train crossing had the arms down and red lights flashing, but the bells must have been disabled. An all-purpose U-Haul was parked on the roadside and a few *Harveys* were helping unload more supplies. I probably shouldn't be complaining about the bodyguard duty. Everyone had to work to make this train go. Staying close to the newly painted sides I didn't need my shield, or at least it didn't make an appearance. Keeping with the generic railcars instead of the brightly colored graffiti we'd used as addresses in the last place we'd hidden.

Grasping the bar on the outside of the engineer's cab I climbed in to see Sadie reviewing maps and codes that would need to be overrode in some areas. Speeds and schedules of other trains registered with the National Transportation Safety Board she would need to avoid. Only this wasn't a car or truck where she could simply take a back road. Trent was explaining the hacks Peyton had put in and her copilot in a way was another *Harvey* with mad computing skills. I'd seen the guy from time to time in the last few months, but never bothered to learn his name.

Having seen older trains in movies, I was impressed with all the bells and whistles this one had. Touch screens were lit up and the cushy chairs could lull a person into thinking they were taking on a choice gig. If it weren't for all the avoid the man issues, you could actually believe you were back in the real world. One where we weren't being hunted just for living.

In the chair Sadie would occupy for the next shift sat a woman. Her hood lined with fur and pulled over her head, hiding her face from me. I believe Riley called her Aunt Cindy, but that seemed a bit familiar for me to call a woman by that name. Especially since my parent's siblings were far from gifted, let alone a *grower*.

"This is Aggs," Trent said once he noticed I was in the small space. He, of course, was who he always was, perfectly sculpted hair, preppy boy on point and another on the train that made me a bit uneasy. "Aggs say hi to Aunt Cindy."

He tapped her shoulder, and she raised her head. Although I did know she was completely deaf, I don't believe that was the reason she hadn't acknowledged I'd stepped into the space. The woman had stepped away from the society years ago. Her only contact the necessary amount to live, her sister and her current nephew. Ms. Weston's twin may have been identical at one time, but pain had aged her, I couldn't exactly say prematurely.

While Ms. Weston had bright azure eyes, Cindy's were a pale lilac. Unlike her twin with chestnut hair, Cindy's was stark white and shorn to the point she was nearly bald. Wrinkles around her eyes were like spider webs or the remnants from lightning cutting through her skin. I wasn't sure if it was the thick coat, but she reminded me of the grandmothers in movies. The ones who have a stocky body, not overweight, but solid yet squishy in a cuddly way.

I needed Breonna or Riley to translate for me. How was I going to learn sign language? Maybe since it was an injury, Summer could heal her.

"Hello," she greeted me. Her hollow, scratchy, voice was distant as if she spoke it from another world with a hint of an accent from a long dead language.

"Hi," I replied, but my head was facing Trent and not her, so she tugged on my sleeve.

She pointed to her mouth.

"She can read lips Aggs," Trent explained, making sure he was facing her and conveying the right message.

"What am I doing?" I asked, trying to remember. Even if my question was for Trent, I had to make sure this stranger was part of the conversation.

"You're going to help her set up each car and she's going to be planting food."

"In each car?" I questioned. "They're dark. What is she planting mushrooms?"

"Sun helps, so does water, but I guess she doesn't need that." Trent gave a shrug. "If my dad wins, we'll be able to do a little construction and put sky lights in the tops of the cars."

"And if he doesn't?" I questioned.

"Then we have two months to figure out what island Riley's mom is going to buy us to hide on."

A loud snort came from Cynthia with a shake of her head.

"See, as long as you face her, you two can communicate."

"Why not call Summer and have her healed before getting me to do this?" I questioned. "What's one day without growing?"

Trent's eyes cut between all of those in the cab before he snagged my upper arm and took me to the space between the engine and the first railcar. A protected space where the wind whistled through but didn't stop. The less than three-foot space made it nearly impossible to not be touching each other and maybe that was his plan. Pledged to Summer didn't mean he was loyal or at least wasn't actively searching for her replacement and for some messed up reason I had made the list. Like I would ever betray the only person who had never wronged me. Then again, I hadn't told her about his come ons so maybe I had in some sense. No matter, at this point my skin was rising and if he didn't step back, there was a very good chance my shield might just make him an indent in the back of the cab. Sadly, for me, the unreliable shield hadn't deemed my unease enough to protect me.

"You do realize the woman is like three thousand years old and has known healers for her whole life, right?" he said as if I'd somehow blurted out an unreasonable request.

"And?"

"And if she wanted to be healed, she could and would have been."

"Sorry I don't have the personal relationship you have with Riley and his mother's twin." I had to rely on tried-and-true methods to get away from Trent and shifted my shoulders to create space.

"It's not that," Trent admitted, letting out a long sigh. "There's a guilt factor with her. Around Vince. Her sister doesn't think she'll allow herself to be healed until he's dead. Even then, she might follow him and kill herself."

The secret council must be including Riley's mom to know that much detail. I'd sat in on a few meetings, but that didn't mean anything. Riley was trying to bring me into a fold where I didn't belong. His mother, on the other hand, with her knowledge, theories were becoming facts. The history of our kind in a way. Never had I considered the fact we were separate from humans. Witches, wizards, mythical creatures, mutants. All on the outs with the so-called normals. Unblessed. *Harveys*.

Now we stood out, younger, age can be guessed, but what about in five years, or ten? This is why they are trying to round us up and mark us. Keep us tracked because we do look just like them. We don't need to only walk at night or have some distinct feature like silver eyes and wings. His mother had lived among the unblessed for thousands of years, with only her sister to be with her. It will take hundreds of years before we even start to truly age. All those behind us in age will start being questioned just like Sadie and the other contiguous.

"Aggs," Trent said, his hand cupping my chin to turn my eyes to his. "You okay?"

"Fine," I replied, steeling myself.

"You can handle protecting her?"

"No, but for some twisted reason, you believe I can." Angling my head created a space between him and me. His hand dropping from my cheek.

"One on one I think you can do great things," he said and my skin crawled.

The politician in him making me uneasy. Sweet talk, closeness brought on by a need or want. All of it not necessary.

I stepped to the side, so I was no longer pinned to the railcar and was free of him. "We're not going to be stopped forever so let's get her started."

Trent banged on the door to the cab and Cynthia stepped out with two huge reusable grocery bags that had seen quite a bit of use. With a hundred railcars, I assume this would take quite a bit of time and I had little to no idea what I was supposed to do.

Maybe it was best that I take Cynthia. Neither of us were exactly chatty so we wouldn't feel offended if we didn't speak to each other. Outside of a clipboard I'd been handed to keep track of what food was growing where, I had no duties. I could simply watch, note, and move on. I should have brought my ear pods so I could listen to music or a book or something. There was no way this wasn't going to turn routine with me chilling out as she worked. How posh and managerial I suddenly felt.

In the first car, Cynthia paced up and down, her mind had to be awash with the reality of what she was being asked to do.

"Many?" she asked and waved along the makeshift wall that separated the pods. Her fingers flying, but I assume it meant something very different to her than me.

Many? Many? When she waved her hand between me and her, I think I knew what she wanted. I held up two fingers and pointed to the end doors and then four for the two in the middle. At least that's the way it's supposed to be in all the railcars. Cynthia simply nodded and dug through one of the bags. Holding up seed packets until she found the one that she wanted. Placing her hand on the far end of the railcar, I stepped to her and tapped her shoulder.

Her eyes cut to me as if my touch had been electric and not gentle. Who was I to tell her how to do her job? I get it, but at some point, there would be a door there.

"Riley and Petra are cutting doors on both ends," I explained, with my phone under my face to help light the dim area so she would be sure to see what I was saying, and her shoulders relaxed a bit. "We're trying to connect the whole train if possible."

She nodded, the lip reading allowing her to know the plan better than what the guys had told her, obviously. Of course, she needed to know more about how we'd be set up and not just step and go.

A girl peeked from behind a door, a *Harvey* one. Her eyes wide as she tried to see what was happening in her dimly lit hallway. Currently, the hallways only had lights powered by a pair of double AA batteries. They stuck to the wall. Between sales and Gil cleaning out stores, we'd gotten just enough for one per car. Not exactly the best option for optimal lighting. For a moment I thought she was in the wrong room when her dark eyes began to glow, only it was a reflection. One that made me turn to see Cynthia's hands glowing as if full of sunshine and vitamin D. The process allowing seeds she'd strewn on the floor to burst forth.

Leaves and vines intermixed along the wall. Sticking to the metal as if there were able to wrap themselves along a stick. The whole center wall filling to the top where they were able to latch on as if she'd been growing for a giant in the sky. Fairytale stories unfolding before me as I thought about Jack and the Beanstalk. Had someone happened upon a grower learning their powers? One who went too far and brought attention to themselves.

One creak of a door was followed by another as a couple of people not assigned to tasks were able to watch a *grower* for the first time. Me too, outside of the propaganda put out by the government, Cynthia was my first to see and the fact she wasn't using pots or dirt confused me.

"Are we supposed to water it?" one of the new girls said as her eyes trailed along with the vines. "My mom and dad always wanted me to go to an ivy league school, not sure this qualifies."

I didn't want to interrupt Cynthia again, but the question was legitimate. What was she growing? Ivy wasn't a food, and I didn't know of any other plant that could survive outside of dirt. Maybe an orchid, but they still balanced in a vase of water. Neither was available in a generic car of pods.

A bright yellow bloom burst forth from one spot and Cynthia's hand cradled it. Nurturing, like a mother with her newborn, as the rest of the vines continued their way along the wall. Soon the petals faded and from the center a green spiky plant grew, elongating until Cynthia had a handful and snapped it off. She passed the cucumber to the first girl with dark eyes and skin smooth with an even tan. Native, I believe, if her stick straight hair being held back by a beaded flower was any indication.

Cynthia cradled the girl's face in her hand and leaned her forehead to her. The moment touching and sweet. Overall, too soon, I believe as Cynthia returned to her plants, waving her hand along the side and causing yellow blooms to burst forth. It was then I noticed the heat in the car. We hadn't moved, so there was no way a forecaster had warmed up one railcar. The warmth came from Cynthia, and I had to wonder about how long it could last.

"They want to know if they are supposed to water it," I asked, speaking slower than she probably needed me to.

Cynthia shook her head and placed her hand on her chest.

"And the cold?" I questioned.

Holding her hand up, she shrugged. "No."

She waved at the girls, and I wrote cucumbers in the slot next to the first railcar. I had so many questions and now I wanted an interpreter because I knew she would be way more verbal than the one word responses barely making their way past her vocal cords. Taking in her features, I tried to see Vince, her son, the one that proved this would be a generational issue if we can't get people to understand us. No longer were we in the dark ages before cell phones, cameras and the internet.

Unlike Vince, who we now know was born in the year one thousand, we couldn't hide for long. At some point, trains had to stop, and we needed to find a place to live in the world. A battle was coming. The only question is, will it be between nations? Or those with and without power?

Could we be left alone? Surrounded by *cloakers* creating a place that didn't make sense on a map. Who would let us be around them? It seemed as if the nations of the world only wanted us to create armies. We heard rhetoric about protecting the country, but others said we were what the country needed to be protected from. But Cynthia and others like her could end hunger, couldn't they? We had a purpose on this planet and if we could show that, maybe they could stop hunting us.

Paying closer attention in the next car, I tried to do more than catch the tail end of Cynthia's power. Wanting to see how it happened. It was almost as if I were watching a child be born. The leaves uncurling upward and roots stretching out along the wall like an athlete pointing their toes to get more distance. Sun bursting from her hands. Warming the car, but not damaging it. The light trickling under the doors of the pods, drawing out the few people not working for the second time.

This time bright green orbs, ripened into the red the size of Cynthia's hand. Tomatoes for the second car and on we went. Green beans, zucchini, grapes, and watermelons. Shaking her head, she kept digging through the bags. Using as many as six seed packets. When we got to Riley's spot, the one where Cynthia would be staying with her sister, we stopped. Letting her settle in for a moment and see the items she brought sitting in a pile across from Ms. Weston's bed.

Her eyes weary, but a smile was on her face as she unpacked a few items. Pictures of her life. At least the life since the invention of the camera. Ms. Weston didn't appear much older than she did now, even though she was dressed in western wear and sitting prim and proper with Cynthia behind her. Unlike the sepia toned images you got when you went to the State Fair and dressed up in old time clothes to pose with empty liquor bottles and fake six shooters. These images were set on a simple background. The faces locked in the serious expressions people had in those times before quick shutter speeds. Edges damaged a bit behind the glass, but the image otherwise perfect.

"Riley stays next door, I think," I said after tapping her knee to get her attention. "I could go on a hunt for Hobbes if I wanted to know which room exactly."

Cindy's eyes lit up as she thumbed through a file folder type box with hundreds of pictures. On her own hunt for something, for sure. Passing me a picture of Riley as a baby, no more than a year, sitting in his stroller. Hobbes, the stuffed tiger toy, still had the tag on its ear, being held tight with his left arm in a headlock while his right hand was pressed to the glass of a tiger exhibit at a zoo. The cat behind the glass pressing its nose to the window.

An innocent enough picture, but I wonder if the big cat knew something about him then. I'd been to the zoo dozens of times and never once had an animal approached the glass the way this tiger was. Staring baby Riley down, head tilted, but not in a way that was threatening.

"You should have known then Hobbes would come on all his adventures," I said, thinking the stuffy didn't look anything like the cartoon he was named after, but that didn't matter. Young boy and his best friend who protected him through thick and thin were live action when it came to Riley and the now tattered stuffed animal.

Cindy took out a notebook that had a pencil tied to it and let out a long sigh of relief. We could communicate better now. Only she didn't start writing. Instead, she tucked the notebook into her reusable grocery bags and slapped her thighs before standing. I guess there wasn't anything she wanted or needed from me. Grasping both bags in one hand, she withdrew a packet of strawberries with the other and stepped out into the hallway. Sprinkling the seeds on either sides of the doors and across along the outer door. I'd become accustomed to her ritual now and was hoping she would let me have the first strawberry. I wondered if they had the same flavor grown from her hands as they did normally. We'd gone to a strawberry field for school one time. I swore the berry was a mix of sunshine and sweet water. Ones from the store were different. As if shipping them in dark trucks robbed them of more than the bright sunlight.

She teased the tiny white flower to give up the fruit growing in the center. Expanding, stretching as the yellow slowly shifted to green, then brightened to a ripe red as she cradled the berry. With barely a twist, it fell from the vine, and she passed it to me. Pinching the green leafed top on the giant berry, I took a bite. Sweetness exploded in my mouth as the flavored juice made me wonder if it was pure liquid in the middle. It wasn't, of course, and even though it took four bites to fully eat the giant berry I couldn't help thinking the treat was gone too soon.

Giving Cindy a thumbs up, her smile widened, and she pulled out the notebook and scribbled *Riley's favorite*.

"I can see why," I replied. "I've always loved the crunch of an apple. You know the hard, but sweet. Something about that snap when you bite it makes it taste better."

Apples for you then. She wrote, then added. *Blessing?*

The question mark letting me know she wanted to know what I was. Trent must not have shared my gift with her.

"I'm a shield, sort of."

Her fingers drew in the air the shape of a knight's shield, then stood as if she had one on her arm in a stance.

"Not really," I explained. "More like a giant bubble that shows up at weird times with little to no control by me."

Her hand stroked my cheek and her eyes softened. The connection and consolation immediate as if she were growing trust in me as easily as she had a vegetable. Warmth bloomed in my chest, a strange sensation I both yearned for and feared. Stepping back didn't offend her. In fact, she seemed to understand completely, as if she knew rejection as intimately as she knew love.

"I'm sorry, I just—"

Shaking her head, she held her hand up to silence me. I'd been around this woman for less than an hour and somehow she could read me. While Ms. Weston was guarded, her sister, who had every reason to be, wasn't. How could Vince torture her to the point she lost her ability to hear and speak? The few strangled words she could express were a step up from grunts from a person with a permanent case of laryngitis and strep throat on the verge of exploding tonsils.

The story Riley told me of what Vince had done to his mother had me holding back tears at the thought. Pouring a molten liquid into her ears and throat some time back in the fifteen or sixteen hundreds to silence her. Not killing her, no he wanted his mother to witness the atrocities he was committing in the name of those of us who were blessed. Back in a time when the few random weird kids in a village didn't cause a full-on government lockdown. The strange hermit living outside the village, not needing to actually come to town often and if they did people parted the seas to avoid them.

These were the ones born before the world was interconnected. I never understood how small our world was until I heard stories of the *elders*. Those *aberrations* born millennia before us. For Cindy, she now knew she'd been born in the year one thousand before the common era. While she may appear middle aged, the woman had seen and lived through more than a history book could hold. Museums shared artifacts that at one time might have actually been a tool or object she used in everyday life.

Elders knew the real story behind the wars and conflicts. The expansion of civilization. Seafaring then and now. They'd seen sickness sweep through a village and antibiotics change the direction as vaccines wipe an illness from the world, leaving only the memory of the symptoms.

Had she seen the library burn in Alexandria? Did she sit in the coliseum and watch gladiator fights? Did she travel and watch the Great Wall of China being built? Was there a great love affair with an artist that was now depicted in oils or stone? How many miles had she walked and was there a part of the world she hadn't explored?

All of it fascinated me, wishing I could sit in the real history class being taught by those who had been there like Ms. Weston and Cindy. Not so much Vince, since the man was a sadist that could put the Marquis de Sade to shame. I didn't want to know how he saw the world, maybe because the mirror of my own life to harsh a reality that would make me second guess my future. Already jaded, the last thing I needed was Vince telling me he had cookies on the dark side for those who join him.

Gathering her items and zipping up her coat, she glanced to the other two pods and pointed.

"Trent, who you've met, lives there with his girlfriend Summer. She's our *healer*."

While the information was requested, part of me wanted to push the healer part. Summer could fix the woman, bring back the sounds of life and open her back up to the world. But Trent's comment about her having the ability to be healed and denying it still made me uneasy. Who searches out a life harder than the one we already had?

"The other pod hosts our security services. I think that rotates," I explained the black uniform wearing super *aberrations* that I didn't truly understand at this point. "This is kinda the VIP spot."

Cynthia smiled, took out a handful of packets and placed them in my hand. She then disappeared back into her room and came out with a hanging shoe rack. It felt wrong to open

Summer's door knowing she was off checking in on people with broken limbs, headaches and anything else she could heal on the fly, but Aunt Cindy insisted and there was no other option. With no lights on in the room, not even a nightlight, all I could make out was the shape of a double bed as Cindy tossed the straps over the top to lock in the shoe rack. Plastic pockets gave me an even bigger front row seat to the magic of Cynthia's gift. Watching the roots explode from the seedlings, seemingly unaware or uncaring when it came to the lack of soil. The nourishment regular plants needed were all provided by Cynthia's ability.

Each herb she planted had extra health properties. I read the back of the packets where they had info spots as she coaxed the plants to grow and before I knew it she had placed the packets, use side out so they could be utilized by Summer in conjunction with her powers. Really, we all needed one of these in each railcar until they were connected. Especially the mint for nausea.

Stepping out of the railcar, snow and wind had completely stopped as the air took on an uneasy thickness. No longer the sharp cold you inhaled quickly, unaware of how it would freeze your lungs. Instead, it was as if a mist had set in like those early mornings close to the equinox back home. When temperatures danced along the mercury, unsure of where to land and the world tried to come to grips with the whole experience. Clouds filled with precipitation trying to decide what form to take and giving into a fog.

Cindy's feet were planted in the snow as if roots had sprouted and anchored her to the ground. Unlike a small plant, open to being transplanted into a bigger or smaller pot, she was a tree. One whose roots run deep and gripped the land for all it could. Fear trickled down my spine but did not cause my shield to pop. Instead, I turned slowly toward a sound echoing through the empty valley. A snarl of warning from eyes locked on Cindy, deep brown with no reflection in them.

My stomach tightened as the empty vessels appeared as holes where the creature's eyes should be. A gray and brown wolf, with ears pinned back, bared its sharp K-9 teeth. Hair raised along the spine with a growl, deep and guttural, between snaps, as others from the wolf's pack stepped in view. The rest being a mix of shades from jet black standing out from the blindingly white snow reflecting the moon to the near camouflaged milky one I only noticed when its head moved. Thick fur, all at attention, letting me know they saw us as a threat and wanted to warn us to leave.

But it was the leader, the alpha, making me wish I had control of my shield. Rubbing my fingers together had never gotten me anything more than a gumball sized bubble and right now I was supposed to be part of the train's protection. The creature was not on a hill and yet we were eye to eye. On all fours, this wolf was over five foot tall. Great Danes were this height. The gentle giants a harsh contrast to the predator letting me know I was on his territory. Fear had spiked. Acid burned up my throat, the bitter bile taste coating my tongue. My mouth arid as I tried to swallow back my unease only to discover I had no moisture. Skin on fire, raised worse than when the ice-cold spray hit me and still no shield.

Cindy's hand landed on the middle of my back, making me jump and flash exploded in front of me. Searing my face like gas being added to a grill. The fire wrapping around me and sending me flying backward with enough force to slam me into Cindy and sending both of us into the side of a railcar. The steel unforgiving, the pressure bursting across my shoulder blades, sucking the air from my lungs before I rebounded. Ice coating my cheeks, forcing me to close my eyes as I face planted in the snow.

CHAPTER FOUR

Lifting my head, a spike of pain shot down from the base of my skull to the middle of my shoulders as if a weight had been placed there. Holding my breath to avoid breathing snow into my lungs, I struggled to move. Around me a mix of gunfire and ear ringing booms tangled with high-pitched yips from the wolves.

Heavy booted feet crushed the ground near me as my hands, palms flat, pushed against the snow below me, compacting the flakes until it became solid enough I could extend my arms. The sick push-up on my knees finally allowing me to breathe in and replenish my lungs for a moment as my hands began to burn from the ice beneath them.

Scrambling, my head swimming from the sudden flight, not the impact, though I couldn't be sure. Gasping, I struggled to not only find air, but words. Crying out, I pawed at the ground, looking for Cindy. Crystals covering my eyes no matter how much I blinked and shook my head. My eyes unable to focus beyond the flakes to the blobs moving toward me. No longer stalking their way through the snow, instead running before being thrown to the side by a second blob.

Rocking back and forth like an infant attempting to crawl, I struggled to push past my crippling anxiety. It appears I had neither the fight-or-flight reflexes needed to respond in this situation. Blame it on the pain now flowing down my back like molten lava. Burning not only my flesh, but layers of muscle. Tendons ceased inside me, causing my back to arch and snap backward. Stretching was no longer an option.

Pain and fear, the two triggers as useless as a light switch during a blackout. No matter how many lashes of pain stung my body, my shield wasn't coming in to save me.

Bringing my arm up to my eyes, I wiped away the mask of snow with my jacket. The numbness in my hands no longer a mystery as my gloveless hand practically glowed crimson. Skin already cracking open as it froze. In the distance at the tree line, stood a dark figure. Watching the melee as the snow was a mix of melting flakes, fur, and blood.

Gun shots had me curling into a ball and covering my head, trying to make myself less of a target. The active shooter drills in grade school weren't useful in this moment because an adult wasn't there to guide us. We were in charge. Desks, closets, options that were all out and, more than likely, the bullets flying weren't for me. They were the wolves attacking us. What was I supposed to do?

"Aggie." Riley's voice cut clear through the cries and howls. "Aggie."

Uncurling, I turned my head to see him running full speed toward me. Dodging people that were engaging in the battle with the wolves. Why weren't they running away? The wolves, not the people. Weren't wild wolves more scared of us than them? All of it strange as I noticed Riley wasn't running so much as leaping forward enough to cross large expanses of space before landing right behind me and skidding across the snow.

His clodhopper size thirteens sent him sideways, unable to find purchase on the now sheet of ice beneath them. The cartoonish way he ran without moving as if a rug was being pulled underneath him, so every step forward was useless as the world moved backward.

"It's Vince," he said once he finally found purchase and landed, knees down beside me. Placing his hand on my back. The fire along my spine splintered into shards as my shield exploded from my back. "He was blocking you. I can only block him for so long."

"This makes sense to you, right?" I questioned, quickening my breaths. Inside my bubble, the reverb buzzed in my ears as we stared at each other.

"I was hoping you got it." Riley glanced over his shoulder and saw his aunt in the snow. "Can you cover the train?"

"With what? Glitter and happy thoughts?" I exclaimed. "I'm not potty trained yet. I just know sometimes when I gotta go."

"You think that might be now?" His eyes widened as I peered through the bubble, the black uniformed people trying their best to keep the wolves at bay in front of me with armed *Harveys* along the top of railcars.

"Why can't you? You have my powers too, right?"

"What can I say? I can't multitask yet." He groaned as he helped me up and moved the two of us in front of his aunt. The indirect shield would protect the woman because I had no ability to expand my bubble. If anything, it was becoming more of an armor, shrinking around Riley and me.

"Can you unblock more than just me?" I questioned because everyone currently was a damn *Harvey* with Vince blocking their powers.

Not taking away their abilities all together, just capping them. At this moment, all outside my shield were lightning bugs in a jar. No matter how strong their glow it couldn't push past the lid. Until I was able to expand her reach, they would stay that way. Much like Riley, I only had so much power. His from being torn in a million directions. Each power a new learning experience as if he were in the Matrix with a thousand files uploaded at once. In theory great, but until he could slow down the world and read the owner's manual, it was clogging the pipeline.

"And leave you exposed?" His words warmed me more than they should. They were friendly, but confusing.

Some part of me wanted for them to be more than him being my friend. Only Riley didn't have that in him, to be focused on only one person, even himself. With every part of him, he searched out helping others. Food, shared, resources, shared, protection, shared. I barely shared my opinion. Helping Riley out when he first arrived came out of a hatred of seeing people being duped. The comparison to my father's Ponzi scheme, see a fool, use a fool. That I couldn't abide.

"Aggs, you need to—"

A high-pitched yip cut him off as a bullet sent the white wolf flying backwards mid leap. The contact a bloom of red below the outstretched paws in his front armpit, piercing the underside of the animal and sending him to the ground. When a plume of snow from the impact settled like dust from a sheet snapped off furniture covered for the winter to reveal the beast was no longer fur covered. The body unable to maintain the shifted form with an injury.

Like Trent, the man had learned to shift with clothes and his puffy white coat had a splattering of black, gray, and red from the mix of powder burns and blood. His platinum blond hair shimmered even in the darkness as the vacant eyes finally showed an emotion. Crawling with only the one good arm, his fingers dug into the ground to pull him along as another elder emerged from the tree line.

"Taylor," Riley called when his oldest friend was brought forth and Vince shoved her toward the new elder.

The girl had been pale before, but in the month since she'd been taken, she'd become translucent. Cheeks sunken in with dark circles under the eyes, the skin clinging to bone because muscle had lost more than form. Her jet-black hair was slicked back, the blunt cut keeping it too short to style, but too long to quaff.

Although we shared cold, Midwestern state roots, her state of dress was miniscule even for the toughest of northern stock. Vince had obviously styled her in the way he preferred. A tight corset bound her torso and lifted her breasts into mounds practically spilling from the top, with long sleeves similar to gloves reaching her shoulders while leaving her neck and chest plate exposed to the elements.

Vince's lips moved, instructing Taylor of her duties, and she took the hand of the other elder. In a flash, they were next to the injured *shifter* as the elder cared for him. A *healer* mending the injured as Taylor used her powers to move them back through the field. Only able to go about ten feet at a time. No longer motivated by Vince's pain strategy to cross the country with Riley and me in tow. Had she brought all these people here? Or had Vince been tracking them? Waiting for our next stop to strike.

Cynthia moved past us in a hypnotic trance. As if somehow her motherly presence would change Vince from the monster he'd become. Had her injury not triggered her to know how twisted the guy had become?

"No," Ms. Weston's voice rang out as the woman tackled her twin to the ground in front of us. "Cindy, you know better."

Cindy's hands flew, fingers twisting in different directions only to be met with harsher, sharp-angled responses from her sister's hands. Ms. Weston clutched her sister's hands and their foreheads pressed together. The women, three millennium old, didn't need sign language to communicate and it had nothing to do with Ms. Weston's ability to *whisper* in people's minds.

The world was slowed, the battle a movie playing out in front of me. Heart pounding in fear for those involved. Never one for action flicks because I got too invested. But how could I not in this situation? I knew the actors. Worse, I was a target. Taylor was halfway to the tree line when Riley stepped away from me. Running toward her as heat seared my spine. The bandage that was Riley's ability to block the *blocker* gone as the world hit me full on.

The noises of battle as people screamed, grunted and those attacking showed how much stronger *aberrations* were to regular humans. The government's fear of them played out in bloodied realism. Those from the train were being lifted in the air. A girl's body was bent backward in front of me. Her scream only quelled when a snap of her spine reverberated in my ears as her lifeless body dropped to the ground like a discarded toy.

Shooting straight up, my hands extended in front of me. A sonic boom sent those in front of me flying toward the tree line, and Vince's face flared with anger. Only Riley was in front of me. The twin elders that were helping us and dozens of Satorians were now tossed with the enemies and I didn't know how to let them back with us. Worse, I feared turning to see if I'd done damage behind me because my shield might go with my gaze. If I hadn't already knocked the train over, I could if I looked.

Behind me the noise of a train powering up meant someone, probably Trent had made a decision. Was he leaving his second in command Riley behind? Had it been made before I lost my damn mind? Do I put my hands down?

Would that shoot me up in the air? I couldn't just not be afraid. My body trembled. Muted voices called to me from outside my shield. Probably telling me something important, but once again I proved I'm not a flyer or fighter. I'm good at being still, frozen, and unsure of myself.

"Aggs," Summer's voice tunneled through my shield. "Aggs, we're leaving."

"Riley, Taylor, they're over there," I called out, hoping my voice could break through like Summer's had.

"Taylor? She's alive?"

"Barely," I called back. "And Ms. Weston, Aunt Cindy and I don't know how many others."

"Then let them through?"

"I don't know how," I cried.

"We have to go," she stressed. "Drop your shield if you want us to save them."

In front of me, my hands were shaking. First frozen, then cracked, now numb yet somehow full of nerves on fire. Pressure built as if the wall were against my palms. My shoulders burned and arms ached.

Vince reached for Taylor, only to have a *baller* hit him from the side. The fire exploded along the edges of my shield and singeing not only my hands but face too. In an instant, I had a weekend's worth of lake rays burned into my skin. The shock jarring and painful enough to have me pull back my hands in pain and cry out.

Summer rushed to my side, pulling me by the train, all the while her hands stroking my throbbing hands. Blisters were forming faster than she could heal as my skin shifted from pink to bright red, then blacken with charring the flesh.

"He's still blocking me," she spat, tossing my hands into the snow.

The contrast of ice making me scream out in pain. Thousands of fine pinpricks stabbed deep into my flesh, sending sharp electrical barbs up my arms. I wanted the pain to end, but when my hands went completely numb, I began to tremble in fear. My arms disembodied from the wrist down. This wasn't the same as when the hand falls asleep. This was the phantom, "where's the limb situation." Was I curling my fingers? Did I have control? Were my hands completely gone? Staring at the snow, all I saw was the arms of my coat disappearing into whiteness fluff. Below that was unknown, and I had no sensation beyond the stinging at my bare wrists.

With a metal grinding jerk, the train moved forward, a horn sounded, and people were running across the field to get on board. Those close by weren't caring which car they got in, and Summer tried to get me to focus.

"Aggs, Aggs, we need to get in a car."

"What about—" the words hollow as the train picked up speed.

We couldn't abandon them. Riley, his family, were across the field. Taylor, already lost to us, was being held hostage. They had nothing with them. How would we find them again? Would the government round them up? The train's whistle called to those in the field, urging them to run faster. Try to use a power and when I glanced backward, I could see it, Riley going back and forth with people, family first, then the rest of them. *Leaping* them close enough, they could grasp the bar on the outside of the railcar and swing themselves inside before he disappeared to snag another person.

"Aggie, now," Summer snatched my wrist, unable to clasp my hand because of the blisters. Or maybe she had grasped my hand and I couldn't feel it.

My feet pounded in the snow as I ran beside the train. Summer released me to grab onto a bar, disappeared inside the car and my lungs began to cease. There was no treadmill to keep me in shape. The jogging Sadie did in the hallway was more physical activity than I'd had in months.

Bright blonde hair popped out of the railcar as the speed increased. Summer's hand reached for me, but I couldn't keep up. Worse yet I wasn't sure I could control my hand enough and surely could handle the pain if I did catch her. Still, I reached out. While I could see our fingers touched for a second, I had no sensation of it as the crowd around me enlarged. Everyone finding a car with someone reaching out to help. The community all trying to save each other. Powered or not, the train was our only security at this moment and if I didn't reach it, I may never find them again.

The center of my chest tightened. Muscles burning as the snow deepened, then plumed around me from the draft of the train choking out what little air I had in my lungs. Only a few of us remained, and I could see the panic on Summer's face.

"I'm trying," I yelled.

"Try harder," she bit.

"Bridge," a person running alongside me cried out in fear.

Ahead of us the track seemed to narrow, but it was more defined because nothing was on either side. Injured or not, I needed to get on the train, even if I wasn't in Summer's car. Any car would do at this point, but I reached for her. Hands held for a brief moment; a slick wetness coated them from the blisters bursting making any hold useless as she fell away.

Crying my name, I watched my feet slowing as she shrunk away. My fight to get on board gone as the train took away my friend, over the bridge and all I could make out was her blonde hair whipping in the wind. Dropping to my knees, my heart clenched around gasping lungs and the hope I had flitted away like the flakes being disrupted by the train's passing.

CHAPTER FIVE

I've determined the abnormal could still shock and surprise me. At least if my scream in terror was any indication. Then again, most would scream if their feet were suddenly in the air as well as the rest of your body.

"You're never going to catch the train if you give up after one try," the *aberration* with his hands under my arms stated. "I swear you youngins give up too easily."

Below me a canyon had been carved out by a river and the bridge the train was crossing had arches to hold up what seemed like mile tall pillars. Once again, I was frozen. Stiff as a board, afraid if I moved, he'd lose his grip on me.

"That your friend?" he asked. "She's the healer, right?"

Was she? Could she be? What was happening? When did we get a *flyer*? Wasn't that just a *leaper*?

"Wow, we could turn you over to the enemies with no fear of you giving up secrets."

The *flyer* tossed me up a bit, and I screamed for the two seconds, or seven hours, it was yet to be determined because time was a construct I couldn't capture at the moment. While I feared he was letting me drop to my death, the reality was I was near catatonic and for that reason, he wrapped his long arm around my front. Holding me tight to him and freeing his right hand to catch the bar on the railcar and fling us both inside.

Spinning out, my feet tripped up when they met land. Summer caught me and my savior in her arms.

"Aggie, oh my God, I thought you'd be gone forever." Tears were streaming down her cheeks and when she released me, she did so with a shove. "Don't you ever do that again. Leave me like that. I won't have it."

"When did you get a *grower?*" my savior asked, having released me and now inspecting a vine full of grapes as if the nightmare he'd rescued me from had been a short commercial break. "This is some old school abilities."

"Stop—where—what? You know I can't—" crashing to the floor, I pressed my back to the wall and curled my knees into my chest. I had no fight or flight, but I did have a good armadillo ball roll in me.

Every part of me hurt and was confused. Which was confusing in and of itself because how can a muscle be unsure? The cramping told the story. My muscles wondering, should I allow her the ability to walk or move? Nah, I'll send her down a path of crippling pain with no relief. I'll twitch a bit too, for shits and giggles. My muscles were jerks and my hands were still undetectable. It was hard to decide if I was falling apart or in a torture chamber of my own creation.

Only relief appeared when Summer took my hand in hers. My arm lifting, telling me of the contact. Tracing the raw skin with her fingers, each pass bringing my hand back in painful stings, then lessening the sensation to a tingle before healing my palm. By the fifth pass, I was able to watch the skin regenerating before me. The rest of me could recover on its own. Muscles needed stretching. Being able to breathe in and out without a stitch in my side. That would happen eventually.

But my hands were back, and I knew where they were without looking at them finally.

Carl appeared from an end room with bottles of water. The younger sibling of the now orphaned set of brothers. Gordon, his older brother, was one of our *movers* and Carl the casualty now growing up a bit too fast. While he's mute from trauma, his heart is so sweet, I wasn't surprised when he offered drinks to all of us.

The *flyer* ruffled the redheaded mop on Carl's head in thanks before picking off two bunches of grapes to go with the water. Offering one bunch to Carl who took it, then went to the open door of the railcar and shoved it closed. Noise now muffled, no longer was the wind blowing past us in a deafening thrum.

"So, that sucked." The *flyer* moved along the doorways, knocking on each one to see if anyone else was in the car. "I'm assuming this isn't your place since little man is here and ya'll aren't taking advantage of co-ed situations."

The man popped a few grapes in his mouth and kept talking.

"You kids." He shook his head and leaned by the light taped to the wall.

His features pronounced a bit, but still young. Was he an elder? Dark, smooth skin showed no sign of acne, but there was a scar. Three to be exact from the top of his eyebrow to right above his upper lip. Jagged, but equally placed. Another elder, holding on to a scar any *healer* could fix. Clad in a long leather duster, with tight black pants and dark Henley. The boots were standard issue, ass kicking ones from the soles, only they laced up practically to his knees.

"Nothing better than groceries on demand," he said, plucking a third bunch off the wall. "Do you two talk? Or just scream at each other?"

"Who are you?" Summer asked, spiking my fear because

59

she was in on all screenings of *aberrations*. Not to mention this man knew quite a bit about us and more than could be obtained in a few minutes of paying rescue hero.

"How do you not know him?" I blanched, pushing back only to come to the realization I wasn't going to be able to push myself through a wall. Even if I did, I'd be falling from a train moving at a pretty good speed.

"I'm Superman. Don't you recognize me?" he joked, standing tall with fisted, well partially fisted, since one hand had grapes, hands on his hips and head turned to the side in full on profile. "I'm missing my cape, that must be it."

Carl giggled. Probably the first time I'd ever heard any noise from the kid.

"Honestly, it got in the way," he continued as he leaned his shoulder on the wall again. "Gave them up before it was popular, maybe I started a trend."

"And by popular, you're talking…" I spun my hand at the wrist to get him to say what we feared.

"Probably around fourteen hundred and something. I mean the nobility of course had their ways, but then again, I avoided Europe for a few centuries. This world is covered in land and still people jammed into one of the smallest continents. We do that, you know?" he said. "Jam ourselves into cities. Living on top of each other."

"Name?" I questioned again, this time finding my feet on the now moving train.

"It amazes me, the whole theory of community. Then again, those that rode in packs tended to hunt those who didn't."

"Name?" Summer said, standing next to me.

"Oh, sorry, undiagnosed attention deficit disorder," he replied, his voice dropping an octave. "Of course, in my day it was called that boy will learn his place."

"Name." both Summer and I barked again.

"Imani." Holding his hands up in surrender.

Summer slapped at his hand when he reached for a fourth bunch of grapes.

"A *healer* with claws." He waggled his finger at her. "I like that. What I like more is living though. I've been tracking this little train—"

"With Vince," I accused.

"Dear lord, beautiful, who hurt you?" he asked. "I stay many steps away from him and his Army of Cretans. Most do."

"Elders you mean?" I asked.

"I can't even be mad. I want to be, trust me," he said, then sighed. "But in the sixties I wore a don't trust anyone over thirty button so I'd be a bit of a hypocrite, wouldn't I."

"Being nineteen hundred and sixty yourself you liked the irony?" Summer mocked.

"You're adorable." Imani slapped his hands together. "That being said. Yes, the whole black don't crack really plays out on us *aberrations*. I should have snuck into your group ages ago, but..."

"You don't believe in communities."

He gave me a shrug with his palms upturned. "I hate dictators more and I've noticed that Vincent has grown a fan club. Even the greatest—" he gagged a bit. "Elders can't seem to get him under control."

"There are others beyond Ms. Weston that are willing to help us?" Summer asked.

"We can only do so much. Something tells me the jerk might just have his claws in politics."

"We have our claws in politics," Summer rebuffed. "Trent Marcus is an *aberration*."

"I've heard the rumors, but there is a candidate running against him with highly favorable polls." Imani tilted his head to the side. "Someone I've seen more than once in my life."

Summer's phone rang, and she quickly moved away to answer it as I kept a safe distance from Imani. He eyed me. Entrancing me in a way as his long arm reached out, and he snagged the grapes he'd been spanked for a moment ago.

"I like you," he said with a discerning nod of his head. "Any idea where or what we're doing now?"

"I don't know. Fly up front and ask the driver," I snipped.

"Do I make you nervous?" he stalked toward me. Dark pools pulling me in as I tried to blink away my fear and unease.

Then again, all elders made me nervous. They'd navigated the world for thousands of years and come out for the most part unscathed.

"What's your name, little one?" he asked, his tone husky, causing all sorts of confusion in my body.

"Aggie," I replied. The name caught in my throat, or was it my breath? Either way, I struggled to form thoughts let alone words.

"Short for Agatha? Agnes?"

Heat erupted through my body as he stepped ever closer to me. What was it short for? Why couldn't I remember? I'd had the damn name all my life and at this point, I was guessing. "Agatha."

"Are you sure?" he asked.

"Yes. I know my own name," I countered, but even I could hear the doubt in my voice.

There were times I wondered if Elders had multiple powers like Riley did. Then again, being drawn to someone wasn't exactly anything more than hormones. Imani may be over a thousand years old, he didn't look it, in fact he barely appeared eighteen and could star in a movie as the love interest any day.

When I first arrived, I was so guarded, I stayed locked away the best I could. Venturing out was an overload to my senses. Having lived in fear of any noise not coming from me, the cacophony of voices, movement and electronics had me practically jumping out of my skin. Slowly, I found myself. Clinging to those who I'd made a connection with and that sent me down daydreaming paths about the future. It was then I realized I too was like any other girl in my high school. No matter how hard I fought it, I had hormones and not on the bad days when a period struck.

Imani was just a man, in my proximity and I was hormone crazed. It would happen to anyone, especially after being saved. Nightingale syndrome. Hero worship. Nothing more. I only wished I knew how to tamp down the reactions. Socially awkward was normal among *aberrations*. Our life was cut short in a way, most of us were locked away. Though to hear the elders speak, they too were run out of towns. The difference being there wasn't a social media post going viral, making it impossible to land in the next town unknown.

"We're going to have to send people back," Summer said as she reentered the space I occupied. "Riley and Tisha are doing a check to see who made it."

"Tisha?" I questioned as a young woman vapored into the space. Obviously, a new *aberration* that passed her powers to Riley.

With box braids pulled back and twisted on either side of her head, then tied together at the back of her neck by a binder. It reminded me of a crown, though I suppose any tiara would be placed slightly behind her hair. Honestly, I'd watched too many movies with ghosts because the fact she was in jeans and a heavy coat threw me off. Shouldn't she be in a long flowy tattered dress?

Unlike Riley clumsily becoming corporeal, Tisha managed the transition with ease. Shifted from vapor to fully formed. About my height, but her heavy snow boots probably gave her a good inch and half. Amber skin, with cheeks a bit darker from probably a mix of the cold and exertion.

"Carl," she said with a gasp, making the little boy's eyes widen. "Gordon is going to be so relieved. He was so worried you'd been on your way back from the bathroom."

Carl gave a thumbs up, then took another bunch of grapes from Imani.

"Seriously, those are for all of us," Summer snapped. "Carl, you're good, but what are you trying to do? See if they'll turn into wine."

"These?" Imani mocked. "No sunshine, these are strictly to be eaten, not fermented. Besides, I'm starving."

"Who is he?" Tisha asked with her phone out, her fingers typing away. "And her?"

"Her you mean me?" I questioned.

"Yeah, I was scooped as the train was rolling out of Satori. Sorry I barely know Summer."

"I'm Aggie," I replied, not sure why I'd be hurt that a girl who I didn't know hadn't heard of me.

"Now Riley will be happy," she said, her fingers typing.

"He will?" I questioned, trying not to be happy he'd spoke of me.

"Pretty sure he was talking about you when he asked me to send him separate texts when I found you."

"Me and who else?" I asked and Tisha glanced up from the phone but kept her lips tight.

"Imani," Imani interjected, saving Tisha from crushing me with Riley's worry over multiple people of the female persuasion.

"Like Cher? Madonna? Prince? Or do you have a last name?" Tisha's lack of enthusiasm when it came to Imani made me smirk.

"Imani Deng." He shook his head. "It's been so long since someone asked, I almost forgot that's important."

"He's not a Satorian," I said and could instantly feel the

bitter taste on my tongue Riley spoke about when he thought of *Harveys*. The second-class citizens. "Not yet anyway."

"Am I growing on you Little One?" he teased.

"Without ointment, anything can spread," I replied, pursing my lips as I tried to not smile.

"You're gonna be my best friend here," he said. "I can tell."

"So, three plus a stow-a-way?" Tisha replied. "Got it. This car usually full?"

Carl nodded, flashed three fingers for the room he came out of, four for both middles and two to the far end.

"Anyone know how many more cars I need to get through?"

Carl held up his hands forward facing then, dropped one and curled in his pinky and thumb.

"Thirteen." Tisha nodded. "Not bad. Hopefully the next car won't have as many people as the last two. It sucks trying to vape in and not hit anyone."

"About that," I said, holding my index finger up. "I have questions later."

"Of course, you do," she replied before becoming a mist and vanishing through the far wall.

Imani did a full body shiver, his head twitching a bit to the side. "Those things have always creeped me out. And you have two of them?"

"No, Riley is an *Amalgam*."

"And that would be what?" Imani asked.

"The one," I replied, as if the weight of his burden was mine to bear.

"No wonder Vince is trying to get this train," Imani said. "And whoever isn't on here, the ones that couldn't catch the train, are being tortured."

Curling my fingers into fists and then splaying them wide had become my distraction. It felt wrong to go into other people's suites without their permission. Even if Carl offered on his own in a way, Gordon and his roommate weren't there.

Instead, I marveled at the way Summer had healed me. My palms had been charred. Jet black like coals dropped from a bag into a grill. Now, there wasn't so much as a healing blister or scar. No damaged skin tightening my hand to make it harder to move. Skin grafted or even so much as warmth, let alone a burn.

"Are you sure you're not a two-month-old Little One?" Imani asked as he sat across from me. Pressed up to a doorway with easy access to the grapes on either side. The fruit vanishing equally on either side. "Your obsession with your hands reminds me of a baby discovering they have toes."

"I basically caught a fireball," I countered. "It stings."

"Still?" he questioned.

"No, and it more than stung when it happened."

"And why did you think catching an inferno was a good idea?" he asked.

"It wasn't so much catching it." I held my hands out, no reason to fear my shield popping out. I was uncomfortable, not scared. "The flames burned along my shield. A half mile away at least, but I could feel them. Their heat and pressure, curving along the edges as if it were my skin."

"It is," he replied. "In a way. An extension of you. Much like our flesh is the final barrier keeping us together. Your shield is the first layer. A thick one."

Part of me was uneasy, but it wasn't as if I had sat down with Ms. Weston to chop up what I was. Riley said she would, if nothing else he needed to learn, too, having absorbed my skill. Who knew how long before we stopped again. If we ever could. I may be stuck on this car with grapes for the rest of my life.

"Why does it seem you have no idea what is going on? Don't you have elders?"

Once again, he choked a bit on the word elder, making me have to hold back a laugh.

"Shield caught in your throat?" he asked, his left eyebrow cocked up before giving me a wink. "Just kidding, there's something about *shields*."

"You know others?" I asked. While I knew others had to exist in theory, confirmation was nice.

"I've crossed paths over the years." He leaned his head back on the doorway, scanning the ceiling where the grapevine continued to crawl as if Cynthia was in the railcar using her powers. His finger pointed and wagged at the growth. "I know you have people helping. Why are you so confused?"

"It's been what? A thousand years since you first took flight."

"Beat those smart-ass Wright Brothers and Da Vinci, though I might have given one of them inspiration."

"Only one?" I chuckled. The stitch in my side finally loosening as tension eased from my body.

"It was a slow millennium," he joked. "They say don't grow up too soon, but we tend to take that to extremes."

"We only have two elders, and one has only been here for a few hours." I popped a grape in my mouth, then waved my hand, still holding a bunch of grapes in a circle. "She's deaf, so I wasn't exactly learning from her. More marveling at all this."

"Cindy?" he questioned. "Is her sister your other elder?"

"Yes, Riley, our *amalgam* is her son, the sister, not Cindy."

"I'm sure after dear old Vince and his collecting ways, I'm not surprised."

"Collecting?" I questioned.

"Jesus, guilt really keeps those two quiet, well Judith quiet, I guess." Imani stretched his long legs out, and they nearly reached the wall next to me. "If I'd seen what they had, I guess I would too. What do you know?"

"What do you know?" I countered. "You're stowing away on our train. Why shouldn't we kick you out?"

"You could try," he laughed.

Nothing worse than making a baseless threat made worse because it was beyond empty. It was idiotic. Like answering a question in class without actually hearing the question and hoping you were right. You weren't and worse yet the whole class was now staring at you as if you were an idiot. Tossing a *flyer* was just letting them go for a ride. He'd be in the next spot ten seconds later.

"Aggie, it appears you need a tutor."

My jaw clenched, and I attempted to glare at him.

"This seems to be one of those carry your own weight to add to the collective places."

"Let me guess, that's a bad thing too?" I reasoned.

"In theory, no, but once you get humans involved, theories are just grand ideas balancing on the edge of failure."

I hated that I liked his dark attitude a bit too much. The idea everyone in Satori was to be trusted had never sat right with me. Then again, Vince didn't exactly prove my worries to be unfounded. Imani held just enough back strangely for me to trust him. Now I needed to find ways to keep his focus for more than a sentence.

"Collecting," I said, circling back. "What is Vince collecting?"

"*Aberrations*," he countered. "If he has one of every kind, then no matter what this Riley kid does, he won't be able to stop Vince."

"It's not just Riley he'd have to fight," I countered. "We'd all protect him."

"In theory." He yawned.

"Maybe we're different than you were," I argued. "Or those who came before."

"Amazes me how each generation says they are different, and still I see the same thing over and over, the only change being the technology."

"You and Vince are from the same generation."

"Yes, but I was still wandering when he lost his love, Lissa." Imani cleared his throat. "Like you said, barely learning my skill."

"Eventually you met up with him," I said, not questioning because he knew too much not to have been around him.

A shiver tore through Imani. "At one time I was part of his collection, not by choice, mind you."

"That where you got that?" I asked, tracing a line down my own face where his scars were.

"Among others."

"You know Summer could clean those up for you," I offered.

"You'd think so, wouldn't you?" he said. "Vince mixes his blood with his punishments."

"His blood?" My eyes widened.

"A trick he learned," he continued. "Healers have tried, but what we've been told until his blood stops flowing Vince's power to block any deep healing persists. Randomly these split open as if the flesh was freshly sliced."

My skin rose and I had to rub my arms to settle it down. "That's why Cindy hasn't gotten her hearing fixed."

"It wasn't for lack of trying, though she did give up sooner than I did. Maybe I was too vain."

"*Healers* can do nothing?" I questioned. "Beyond that?"

"Not really. Cindy grew aloe and herbs to make a salve to soothe me when I escaped." He closed his eyes for a moment. "For years she took any in that escaped when Vince was high

69

in his castle. Then it became a trail of broken people until she no longer could deal with the destruction her son wrought."

Imani was no longer in hyper mode. Instead, the reflecting back on the time with Vince had him reliving trauma. I'd only had a few days around him. How much time had Imani been with the sociopath?

"Eventually he lost power." My words strained a bit as they tried to escape my lips.

"Back to your lessons. You will learn nothing from Vince's idea of fun," Imani said, popping out of the PTSD flashback stealing him from the here and now. "Where should we begin?"

"How many empowerments are there?" I asked. "If Vince wants a full collection how many more of us will he need?"

"Haven't checked his stock. You were burned, your friend is a *leaper*, and we know all *shifters* are drawn to him like the sick little puppies they love to embody."

"Not all," Summer said coming out into the hall with her phone glowing and highlighting her face.

"You have one then?" Imani asked. "A *shifter*?"

"Yes, Trent Marcus," I replied, a bit uneasy when I gave up his name. "He also rarely turns into a wolf."

"And he's the last one to stand up for Vince," Summer protested.

"Of course," Imani responded, but in a way a bit patronizing. As if he saw naïve children unable to understand the way the world actually worked.

Would I be as dark when I'd lived a thousand years? If I lived more likely. I'd overheard Riley arguing with his mother about trusting his friends. No one was to be trusted, according to the elders. Only Riley didn't believe that. The optimism of youth had to come from somewhere beyond inexperience. Lord knows I'd experienced enough to believe in the evil of man and most days I did, but Riley had changed me. He'd

70

come back for me, well, Taylor and I, but still I'd never had anyone besides Summer come back for me and part of me questioned her motives. Maybe Peyton had described me from one of his visions and that's why she reached out. Best friend or not, there was part of me that wondered if we were friends for the simple fact that her mother didn't want her to be my friend.

"History lesson," I said when I realized I had an expert, somewhat trapped and in the mood to speak. "Why didn't *aberrations* come together in the past?"

"The *Harveys* of the world wouldn't like it," he said. "One or two unusual people sure, but a group, that was a threat."

"*Harveys* are people born in the year two-thousand," Summer corrected. "Without powers but cursed in their own way."

"Guilt by association," Imani reasoned, and let out a long sigh. "Another reason we don't congregate even when drawn to each other."

"What do you mean?" I asked. "Drawn to each other?"

"Is it really that complicated, Little One?" he asked. "Weren't you all pulled into some mystical cave of wonders not that long ago?"

A shiver tore through my body, causing me to jerk a bit to the side from the memory. My shield triggered, making me wonder if it appeared when the nightmares came in the middle of the night. Imani, unphased by the bubble of protection around me cocked his head to the side as Riley misted his way through the wall, sliding across the floor from the running leap he'd made to get through the rail cars. The ghostly form not tripping over my feet, and he worked to become corporeal and using his hands to stop himself at the end of the railcar.

"Now that was interesting," Imani said.

"We just had a *vaper* come through here," I replied, a bit confused.

71

"Not his power, but the fact he slid through your shield."

"He was mist, he slid through a steel wall," I said. "Two actually."

"You really don't understand how strong your shield actually is, Little One." His dark eyes peered into mine. "Or how much control you actually possess."

CHAPTER SIX

"Ugh, finally," Riley said, bent at the waist and gasping for air. "I really need to run with my mother more. Summer, can't you just touch me and make me like an Olympic athlete?"

"Factory standard," she said. "Sorry, your DNA may have glitches that can be repaired and all, but I'm not a miracle worker."

"That would be cool, turn us all into super soldiers," Imani said. "Alas, even the gods of old had limitations. Seems a shame because what is the use of being a god if you can't do it all?"

"Maybe to learn to work together," I replied, this time feeling my shield fold into me as if my skin was tightening for a moment with a hug.

"Who are you?" Riley asked, his eyes cutting to Imani.

"Not this again," Imani whined and lolled his head back against the door. "Honestly, can't you all send out a group text or something updating the team of new members."

"No one said you were a new member." Summer cut her eyes at Imani, obviously not forgetting or forgiving him for the *shifter* remark. "Right now, the last thing we need is another elder around."

"I get it." Imani stood, stretching his long arms, his fingers touching the ceiling and not because he was pushing up on tipped toes. "The few you've taken on haven't exactly been useful."

"Pretty sure your full belly would contradict you," I said, pushing up from the floor since I was the only one sitting and as much as the thought of curling into a tiny ball appealed to me, that wasn't my power.

"Full? Even if these grapes had been fermented and aged in a barrel, I wouldn't be so diluted to believe I was full." His long index finger flicked a leaf on the vine. "That being said, Cindy is useful. Any chance there's an orange tree somewhere? The cold air is giving me a little tickle in my throat."

"Okay," Riley said, holding his hands out and shaking his head a bit. "As much as I'd love to be caught up on this." His hand moved up and down in front of Imani. "I came here for a reason."

"Oh, do tell," Imani prodded. "I so love a good task."

"Yeah, don't know you, your powers or how you know my aunt so right now we have bigger issues."

"Look at him." Imani clapped. "Judith's son is taking to his task of the savior and damnation of us all with gusto."

Riley rushed or leaped. It was hard to tell the difference when the kid had the ability to travel long distances in a fraction of a second. Either way, Imani was now pressed to the door with Riley's forearm crushing his throat. Imani's eyes darkened, as if the pupils were now filling the space once reserved solely for the whites of his eyes.

Amalgam or not, Riley wasn't exactly the best at using more than one power, and Imani was built like an Olympic athlete. It could be because he was a grown man to the pubescent teens we were. Either way the millennium age gap

74

had Imani overpowering Riley and twisting his arms behind his back in such a way Riley dropped to one knee before him. Turned and facing me, the swift movement caught even me off guard.

"Tell me something, is this how you greet all new people?" Imani asked, his voice a deep growl at this point. "If so, I might need to have a talk with dear Judith about her ill-mannered offspring."

"Let him go," I bit as if somehow in the half hour or so we'd spoken I had reached a level worthy of controlling the elder.

"I'm a bit surprised you let me touch him at all," Imani said, with Riley's arm pointing skyward in opposition of his body being angled down. "Why aren't you shielding him now? Sending me flying as you engulf him in protection, Agatha?"

"I don't know how." My voice trembled, and I hated myself for it. The trembling, the shaking and the fact I no longer felt my shield holding me tight. Instead, my skin was raised in alarm. Gooseflesh amplified the cold rushing across my flesh in tiny pinpricks at the end of the follicle.

"Then you need me to stay," he said, finally releasing Riley with a shove and holding his hand out, his fingers pointed. "Never rush me, boy. *Amalgam*, chosen one, Judith's pride and joy aside, I will do my best to end you."

Riley's eyes narrowed, but he was Judith's child, and she did not raise a fool. Of that I had learned. Normally, he was one to be metered. Then again, the last elder who knew his mother had tried to sacrifice him in an ancient tradition. But I wasn't one to question family dynamics, since the few cousins I knew were distant and might as well be strangers. I doubted I rose any type of emotion in them, let alone the urge to kill me.

"You can train her?" Riley asked, the worry and wary in his voice evident.

"I can educate her. Something tells me there has little to no formal training here." Imani tugged on the lapels of his leather coat. More to straighten out and smooth the garment to right himself. "Now, were you passing through, or do you have a purpose here?"

"Wow, I'll have you know I'm the Vice President in Satori."

I did my best to hold in my smile because I knew Riley hated that title. Unless something had shifted in him, the last thing Riley wanted to be was in charge. If he could, he'd toss away all his *Amalgam* powers and save his favorite one. Though I'm not sure which one that could be.

"That and a few coins will help you take a piss in Europe, beyond that, sorry it means little to anyone else." Imani scanned Riley. "Unless you're trying to be like your cousin. If so, I grieve for the kid who would be king here."

"Ignore him," Summer said, reaching for Riley to pull him away from Imani whose focus returned the grapes, though the draw to eat them must have passed. "What's going on?"

"Petra, Gordon and I were going to try to connect the cars while the train is moving," he said. "We figured if Aggs could put her shield around us—"

"Whoa!" I exclaimed. "What, like some bubble you guys can function in?"

"Well, yeah." Riley shrugged, as if it would be no big deal. "Petra on one side, me on the other, cutting the doors, then insert the passageway. I could float through to the next one and so on."

Insane, the boy had gone mad with power and thoughts of his own abilities. That made sense. Me creating a bubble of protection at eighty miles an hour, no, that was a bit more on the loco side for sure. I pushed past them. Finally taking Carl up on his offer as I went in the room and sat on the bottom bunk I assumed was Gordon's. Head resting in my hands, my fingers curled into my hair, scratching at my scalp.

This was insane. The logistics alone were ridiculous and besides, we were going to need to stop from time to time. Which means if the train is being tracked by Vince, we might as well buy that island and set up a perimeter to fight off Vince and his thugs instead of keeping this insane railway to nowhere going.

What was the point? Let's clear it out and start over. Or just drop the whole communal idea. Maybe Imani is right. Community is BS and we're better off on our own. Depending on people—no forget people depending on me was crap. I wasn't exactly the best person in a crisis. Protecting me, sure, but my shield was only enhanced because Riley boosted me.

A small hand on my shoulder made me jump and when I looked up from my palms, Carl was giving small pats of comfort.

"I'm good, little dude," I said. "I just wished people would understand the superhero stuff doesn't really apply to me."

He held his hands apart as if there were a baseball there, then expanded it further, more dodgeball size. When he held his hands wide, I got the picture. It was when he brought one hand sideways in front of his nose, then took his pointer finger to press in the middle of his palm, then swooped through the air to the backside of his hand that I lost track of what he meant.

"It's been years since I saw that," Riley said from the doorway and Carl dropped his hands to the side.

"That sign language?" I asked. Riley had been teaching Carl a few words to make it easier. The kid wanted to communicate but was stunted by a block Summer couldn't break. Not with a thousand hammers or hours of healing. The kid needed therapy and none of us were qualified.

"No, but it was something my grandmother used to say when I was little." Riley stepped into the room. "My father's mom, obviously. Instead of holding her hands out wide saying I love you this much, she held her hand up to her face."

"And that means?"

"I love you from the palm, around the world and back. Her arms weren't wide enough to show me how much she loved me."

I looked at Carl, sure that he wasn't telling me of his undying devotion to me. Small ball, bigger ball, wide arms… I flashed to when I first played with my shield. Alone in my room, where no one could see. Expanding my hands and not knowing what the transparent orb was. If there was anything more than electricity and my imagination. We all thought we were imagining things back then. The fairytales and games you play as a kid. Where the floor is lava, and a bath towel is a cape. At times for a superhero, other times because you were a queen with a plastic crown and bejeweled heels.

When I was Carl's age, my father was my hero. This grand man who could do no wrong. Babysitters had powers, catching me when I was doing something I shouldn't because of their honed hearing and unease when I was silently trying to sneak something.

The last thing I wanted to do was let Carl down. I could only imagine how cool it was to be surrounded by people with all sorts of powers at his age. The world of make believe wasn't for him. Reality, the abnormal common place.

Imani stood behind Riley, and I got it. The world was small to Imani. It had been so long since he believed in the wizard and the stories trying to explain the strange phenomena in the world were about him and his contemporaries. The world had magic, but the magician was no longer amazed with the vanishing act because he knew where the trapdoor was and understood to watch the other hand.

"Explain this insanity to me again." Letting out a long

sigh, I hoped I could breathe in enough air to stop the spinning making my head light.

———

"It doesn't work that way," Imani explained when Riley asked if he could turn me into vapor, too. "While her powers can be added to yours, she's a shield. That's it, nothing more nothing less."

"But when I touched her back, didn't her powers and mine combine to make her shield bigger?"

Imani pulled in his lips, his eyes moving between Riley and me as if calculating a formula.

"*Amalgams* are weird. I've never heard of one using more than two powers at one time and that was more out of self-preservation. More than likely, Aggie likes you."

"Wait. What? You know you shouldn't—" My face burned as Imani raised his hand to silence me.

"Okay, I meant as a friend, but if you're gonna protest like a kid sneaking chocolates—"

"I wasn't protesting," I countered, even as my stomach tightened and flipped. My hands clasped together as I squeezed a bit tight.

"They are cute together right," Summer gushed.

Waving my hands as if that would somehow clear the air. I moved out into the hallway to escape as I eyed the outer door, wondering would my shield be like a giant hamster ball if I jumped off the train? Anything to get away because once Summer started her dream of side-by-side picket fences and family vacations like the world wasn't sideways, I might never get her to stop. People didn't marry their high school sweetheart and we weren't even in high school.

"Ya'll are gonna need my help if we want to make this

work," Imani said. "And we're getting back on track before people start sitting in a tree together."

The sing song tune instantly rang in my ears. K-I-S-S-I-N-G, first comes love, then comes marriage—

"I'll fly Aggs. You do the ghostly thing just let me know where to drop her."

"Wait what?" I protested as the door opened and cold air blew through the railcar. A mix of winter and speed. Outside, the train wasn't going at a lolling pace. No, we had to be going at least sixty if not more.

"You did fine last time," Imani said.

"Last time! Last time!" I blanched with my hand extended to the door. "Last time I was caught by surprise and thought I was being carried to my death!"

"Now you know better, Little One," Imani said as he booped my nose like a child. "Have we not become instant best of friends? Do you not trust me with your life?"

"I don't trust *me* with my life. Why the hell would I trust you?"

"It's best to scoop and go. I'll have Petra open the door of where you need to take her," Riley said as if I was supposed to—

The air swirled around me with a deafening whoosh. The sun rising as if chasing the train. Basic physics had us a dozen cars down the moment Imani snatched me and flew out the door. While swinging around, I tucked my head into his chest. The smell of cloves and well-worn leather enveloped me. His arm held me tight around my waist as I held the scream in and clung to him like a koala bear clinging for dear life.

What happened to holding hand in hand with Superman as they flew through the night sky? Oh right, only two *flyers* could do that. His power did not cross over to me. Lesson imparted through fear, circumstance and sheer unyielding life. Why can't life give a yield sign just once?

"Oops," he said and once again the world swirled, my body registering the change in elevation and speed. The swooshing through the air had vertigo sending me over the edge. Having literally no idea of where I was, how high or with what I assumed was a deep dive, low I possibly was.

Eyes practically plastered shut, afraid of whatever had made him say oops. Nothing good came from oops. Bad things like the train got away. If I was lost, I was lost. No reason to turn back now. Even if I knew we were turning back a bit. Where was my shield now? I was scared stiff and once again, Imani had shut the thing down.

A hard jerk unlocked my legs from around his waist and a spin had me stumbling when my feet discovered ground existed again. I tumbled and rolled as a mix of strange hands reached and grabbed at me causing my shield to send four guys in different directions—slamming into walls and one letting out a loud scream, that vanished, sucked into the vacuum created by the train moving. It pulled my heart and soul with it, like Ursula removing Ariel's voice.

"Gordon," Petra yelled, and I opened my eyes to see Imani disappearing out the door.

"What happened?" I panicked, my heart thudding in my chest. "Gordon? Where's Gordon?"

The normally pale, red head was nearly translucent when Imani flew back in, this time slamming into the wall across from the door as Petra shoved the door closed. Gordon's lips were pursed, and eyes closed. If it weren't for the mop of hair on his head, he could have been a marble statue.

"Is he?" I asked, dropping to one knee, afraid to finish my question as if that would make him less dead as my fingers ran through the tangled hair.

"Scared?" Imani replied. "Yes, but really, your parents were much too nice to you growing up."

"Yeah, we weren't tossed off running dinosaurs like you

were," I snipped. "Gordon, please Gordon, say you're okay."

"You're okay," he grumbled, his head moving slightly to the side. "I'm in the middle of a nightmare and I wish someone would wake me up."

"Should we tell him?" Riley nudged Petra, who was just as lost as I was in the moment. "That he's late for biology class and really should put on clothes."

"Not funny," Petra spat. "This is getting to be too much."

The normally calm Jacob Petra was starting to break down. Our whole community was. Outside pressure was one thing, but at least we knew our enemy. The kid with laser beam eyes, currently had his dark hair tamped down with a backwards ball cap and tanned skin was visibly exhausted. Not that I blamed him, we all were and seeing his best friend be flung around wasn't helping the situation.

"My bad," Riley said as if twenty minutes ago he wasn't in flip out mode. "Look, we only have so much time. Stopping from now on isn't going to be an option, at least not like it has been."

"I get it," Petra said shaking his head. "Doesn't mean the guy shouldn't take a minute to realize he didn't die."

"I didn't," Gordon whined and rolled on his back. "Damn it. That means I have to work with you two a-holes and old sugar tits?"

"What the hell did you just call me?" I bit ready to stomp on his ass.

"An a-hole," he replied.

"I'm sugar tits," Riley said with a shrug. "More than likely."

"I thought Gordon was the shy quiet one of the group?" I questioned the kid I never really knew. I knew Carl better, and he didn't speak.

"This is what happens when he gets time off and isn't spending all day stacking railcars with his brain." Petra finally

82

relaxed and sat back for a moment. "The whole first world problem of having time off."

"Who threw me out of the car?" Gordon asked with his hands stacked and resting on his forehead and eyes closed. "More importantly, who saved me? How? What just happened? Is it best I not know?"

"Oh, Aggie and her glitchy shield tossed you." Riley thumbed at me as if I hadn't told him a thousand times, I don't know what the heck I'm doing when it came to my powers. "Imani has some superhero complex and decided to not let you die."

"What a man won't do for a Klondike bar." Imani shook his head.

"What's a Klondike bar?" Gordon asked and Imani went into an explanation of the commercials that had been on for decades.

All of it white noise because my own thoughts were catching up to my reality. Words, swirling winds and howling calls. My mind compartmentalizing every bit of what was not only asked of me but done to me. Rage bubbled up inside me, my fists clenching as I slowly rose.

My fist flew, crashing into the side of Riley's face, catching him mid laugh with his buddies.

"Just scoop and go—isn't that what you said? Like you somehow know how to deal with me." He righted himself just in time for me to shove him backward and send him tumbling.

"It worked, didn't it?" he countered.

"Is it wrong that I'm enjoying this?" Imani asked the other two behind me when Riley caught both of my wrists.

"You would have never said yes." Riley's eyes locked on mine as I fought back tears.

"That doesn't mean you just do it to me," I snarled as I struggled to break free of his hold on my wrists only to have Riley press me to the wall.

"This is about you flying with her, right?" Gordon asked.

"Maybe I missed something," Imani said. "God, I wish I had popcorn right now. How long have they been a thing?"

"We're not a thing," Riley and I said in unison, only to get a mix of knowing glances between the other three guys. "We're not."

"Jinx," Imani said, then checked with Gordon and Petra. "Isn't that the word?"

Pushing against Riley's hold, he finally released me, and I shook out my wrists. A mix of hurt, both physical and emotional, hit me. Part of me wanted Riley to correct me. If he'd had contradicted me, I could have pointed out he was a horrible boyfriend that had been ignoring me. Even a crappy date that never called back. Instead, he'd confirmed ghosting wasn't just his new superpower.

Groaning, I wished I did have control of my shield so I could raise my hands and pin them all to the wall. A few *Harveys* peered out of the center suites. Watching the show, one of them snapping off bites of a piece of licorice. Even in our own world, we were freak shows. Entertainment for bored children having been dragged to a zoo for a school trip. We were basically the screaming red butted monkeys at this point.

"Can we do this?" I asked, finally wrenching away my arms and rubbing my wrists to remove any sensation left behind by Riley. If nothing else, Imani would be leaving once the guys got sucked out of the train when my shield failed, and I could get another round of entertainment.

Riley gave me a curt nod before becoming incorporeal and disappearing through the end of the railcar. The opposite end of the railcar already had the accordion style throughway attached. They wouldn't need me for a few minutes as the railcar lit up from Petra's mad welding skills. No matter how practiced he was, they still needed the door secured by what appeared to be giant suction cups. Gordon had placed them, then stepped away. At some point, he'd be the one to heave the steel plate to the side as easily as I would flip a page in a book.

Wandering to the opposite end of the car, I noticed, while attached securely, the connecting floor swung like an old rope bridge. Leaping might be the preferred method once all the cars were connected. Placing my hands on either side of the opening, I saw through a half dozen cars. No one was rushing or moving among the newly opened cars. Not that I blamed them. At the end, I noticed a door. Traditional with a knob and locks. Who would be willing to stand in the center long enough to turn a key? Insane people that I know. More than likely it was Peyton's suite or suites. Housing electronics set for monitoring the outside world and letting us, while limited, communicate with each other.

Pressure on my hips shocked me a bit less than before as Imani helped me to the next car. Not so much flying me as pulling a ballet move as he stepped, unafraid, through to the next car.

"Scoop and go?" I questioned.

"You seemed a bit hesitant to step through." Imani said, his voice soothing and hands warm having not released my hips. "I was tasked with moving the connectors through."

"Couldn't Gordon lift them all at once?" I questioned, noticing stacks leaning alongside walls for at least a dozen cars. "And without leaving where he was at?"

"Probably, but he gets distracted, plus these aren't exactly open space," Imani explained, spinning around me, but maintaining a connection with his hands on my hips until he was on the front of me. His hand smooth as it trailed a bit of warmth around my waist before releasing. "More of a threading the needle which for movers isn't their specialty."

"Stacking solid bricks into a pyramid in the middle of the desert," I reasoned. "Open air, no real fine skills."

"Ask them to toss a semi-truck down the street, no issues,

85

through a window..." Imani held his hand flat and moved it back and forth. "There's a fifty-fifty, no, more forty-sixty, actually probably ten percent chance it'll hit that window. Going through it even less."

"Then I guess he won't be the one we use to launch our nuclear missiles."

"Probably a good idea."

Imani lowered the corridor onto its side and then pushed it through. Creating a thud once it was in the railcar I'd just left and no longer had walls to hold it up. Five were in this railcar and as I helped with the second one I wondered, why couldn't the others, hiding away in the suites we were passing do this? Starting a bucket brigade as it were. There was no reason for Imani and me to move all these down and soon even I couldn't help him. Wasn't that the point? Sure, only Riley and Petra could do the laser welding trick, but this was basic. I held my hand up as Imani moved to the third one to stop him.

Determined, I began knocking on doors. None of the suites opened up. *Harveys* were supposed to earn their keep. Heck, even the *aberrations* in the end suites could do a little heavy lifting. It wasn't asking too much. Peyton was probably the only one along this back half of the train actually working.

"Not every door can be answered," Imani said.

"Is that some deep philosophical belief passed down directly to you by Plato or something?"

"How old do you think I am?" he scoffed. "And no."

"They're in their rooms. Where else could they be?" I snapped, pounding with the side of my fist now.

"Let's see, you were attacked, and most of the people were in some way outside helping fight and you all had to run to the closest opening."

"And you're saying no one made it to the last dozen cars. If anything, that is where they should end up."

"Maybe, but outside of the handful of people in the first

car, have you seen any movement?"

It was eerily quiet. I'd give him that. A ghost town like when we were leaving Satori. Expecting to see people running up and down, cutting through the lobbies of our suites. Abandoned and alone, with only a few cars left in place. The once five story container living, reduced to a few rows as the others had been moved to actual train tracks. Rubbing my upper arms, I attempted to quell the gooseflesh to no avail.

"Do you want to go and snag those people huddled in the other car?"

"Probably." The cold continued to creep down my spine. "Tell me something, Imani."

"Agatha. There is an old phrase, ask me no questions, I'll tell you no lies."

"Are we busying ourselves for no reason?"

"What do you mean?" he questioned, patting the next corridor to be moved with his hand, letting me know it was going to be done with or without other people's help.

"Is it pointless?"

"I'm over a thousand years old," he said, a tone to his voice different from before. No longer wistful, instead ancient and knowing. "And I've yet to find the meaning of life."

"You're useless." Shaking my head, I had to wonder if this was basic homework. The worksheets given in class to keep us occupied and not really learning.

"And yet, I'm being tasked with a project."

Lowering the corridor, he took on most of the weight and when we went to push it through, I noticed the other ones had been moved. The *Harveys* were taking up without being asked. A small spark of satisfaction bubbled inside me.

"Look, the world spins, seasons change, babies are born, and people die. We eat, we drink, read a good book and if luck snuggles a bit close to a person for a time."

"Just snuggle?"

"You're a kid," he replied. "I would feel a bit pervy if I said anything more."

"I know what sex is, trust me any friend of Summer's knows the ins and outs." I shook my head, wishing I didn't have the gushy memories of Summer explaining what I'm told was the most magical connection known to man. While my body reacted and warmed, if nothing else, the hurt from Riley's absence and now rejection had me confused.

"Please, read a good fresco from Rome or check Indian sculptures around temples and you'll know that." He scanned me. "You've really been sheltered, haven't you?"

"By age twelve, the government was trying to lock me away for experimentation," I replied.

"Before then?"

"My father was put in jail for running a Ponzi scheme when I was eight."

"All I hear are excuses to avoid living," he mocked. "I swear you youngins don't know how good you have it."

"Right, because we can just fly to the next village, and no one knows we're freaks. Oh wait, that's your generation."

"Aggs," Petra called, and I made sure to shoulder bump Imani as I passed him, only to stand petrified at the opening between the railcars.

"At some point you're going to have to channel your fear," Imani said, and I looked over my shoulder at him. "You're focusing on controlling your shield. It's the strongest when anger and fear are overwhelming you."

"And?"

"You've never really tried to bring it out on a sunny day, Little One."

"Why would I need it then?" I asked, even I could make out the fear in my voice.

"Besides the fact you'd burn from the sun's rays? Bad things don't just happen in the dark."

CHAPTER SEVEN

Fear and anger. Well one of those emotions was thrumming through my body as I stood, staring at Riley across a divide as wind stung my eyes. The rhythmic sound of the train wasn't so even on the outside. Hard clanks and random jerking from side to side might not be felt inside the railcar, but when you looked down and saw the steel, and slightly rusted links, you became very aware of the world around you. Jumping over a corridor link didn't seem as stupid at this point.

"You can do this, Aggs," Riley assured, holding his hand out to catch the plank being passed to connect the two railcars temporarily.

When did we become tightrope walkers? More importantly, can they hear my heart beating? I'm pretty sure at this moment I understand how Indiana Jones felt in that movie where the man tried to pull his beating heart from his chest. Can your own heart break your chest bone? Pressure is building there and I'm not a hundred percent that it won't snap every bone and burst from my rib cage.

Before being fully locked down, I remember learning about involuntary and voluntary muscles. The heart you could learn to slow down, but never stop. Much like the lungs. Holding your breath only lasted so long before they demanded to move again. Similar to a kid with ADHD, with no medication after three *Red Bulls*. Oh, they'd try to be good, twitch a bit, but eventually they'll knock you out to do what they want to do. Move in and out.

Mine were currently working on the knocking me out stage as my head fogged over a bit and I needed to brace myself on the edge of the opening. A sharp sting trans versing my palm once I made contact with the metal I now knew had been left with a razor's edge to help with the connection. Knowledge did not have me pulling back my hand. Nope, I was the dumb kid trying to figure out the painful sensation on a hot stove.

Blood trickled down my arm, catching on my sleeve and darkening the gray material. The pain and panic setting in as my hand moved from the metal, but not because I'd pulled it away. Instead, it was moving as my shield appeared around my hand.

"There you go," Riley said. "Now turn and make it bigger."

"That's what she said," Gordon chuckled behind me, and I missed the shy guy who was overworked.

"Knock it off," Riley replied. Extending his hand to mine, he leaned across the opening.

My hand reached out, blood pooling on the bottom of the bubble around it as he reached through and grasped my hand. Tugging me gently toward the open space and letting me tap my foot a few times on the thin plank. Probably eight or nine inches across, but barely an inch thick. Behind me, Gordon had a foot bracing the end and I noticed Riley was doing the same. Anchoring the wood. At one time I was in gymnastics. The beam was half this wide and I was half as tall as I was now and still the fear of falling off had my shield growing around me and my question of would I turn into a hamster ball answered. More rolling across than stepping either way, I made it.

Riley was enveloped fully in the sphere as his hand stroked along the slice in my palm. For the second time in less than a few hours, my hand was being healed. This time I watched as the skin stitched back together, leaving a slight line for a moment before returning to the fresh layer. Untarnished beyond the blood drying on my hand.

"Now Gordon needs to set up the corridor. We need your bubble." He pressed his forehead to mine and dropped his voice low. "I know you're scared and nervous. You have back up. This is just a really weird training room."

"This is on-the-job training, Riley. The kind that can get someone killed."

He turned me around, lifting my head to see Gordon waiting with Imani behind him.

"People are trapped in the cars behind us. With only myself and Tisha, to let them know we're fine. We hadn't even gotten the food served when we were attacked."

"You know I don't care about people, right?" I tried to joke, but the words came out a bit choked.

"Gordan's a good guy, so put the shield around him."

Shaking out my hands I stepped to the edge. The plank had been removed and Gordon was holding up the corridor with a slightly annoyed face. I get it, it may not be heavy to him, but it was awkward and needed to be extended before Petra could attach it to the doorway.

Even if Gordon was being a brat now, his brother was quite a few railcars away, putting on a brave face. Honestly, the only way I knew to get my shield at this moment was fear or pain. Empathy for his brother made me want to cry, not burst forth with my shield. Fear it was. Breathing in deep, I stepped back five paces than ran. Extending my hands to the side once I leaped and my shield filled the space between. The hamster ball in place, I stared at Gordon and held back my tears.

Who cries when they're scared? I do. Scared, frustrated, trapped. If that wasn't my current situation in a nutshell, what was? Gordon used one hand to hold up the corridor and extended his hand only to have it snap back once it hit my shield.

I was trapped. There was nothing underneath me but the steel rails, gravel and wood rail ties. The link jostled a bit, bouncing back and forth even though we were in a straightaway. My shoulders burned from extending my hands out to the side as I stood suspended in the air.

"Can you get in?" Gordon called behind me to Riley, but I wasn't going to turn and find out his answer.

Who needed to turn when pressure pushed on my spine followed by an 'ow' from him. Question answered. Imani stalked up the hallway. Moving around the *Harveys* to stand directly behind Gordon. His eyes, dark vessels guiding me even before he spoke.

"Hey there," he said softly.

"Hey."

"Whatcha doin'?"

"You're a comedian now?" I snipped.

"All week and twice on Sunday," he said and moved in front of Gordon. "You want to let me in?"

"Sure, is this like the whole vampire thing? I just need to say yes?"

"No, here's what I need. Close your eyes and listen to my voice."

My eyes snapped shut quickly, wishing the nightmare would be gone once I stopped hearing the whooshing around me. Only it didn't stop.

"Remember the little kid," he said. "You can't start small because this shield is already a good size. You like geometry?"

"Does anyone like geometry?" I asked. "Why are you frustrating me?"

"You know the center of a circle?" he asked.

"Sure, I do."

"Your heart is the center," he explained. "The further out you push from the center, the bigger your shield is."

"Can I derail the train?" I asked.

"Do you want to?" he questioned, and I opened my eyes, only to be chastised. "Shut 'em."

"If I extend equally, wouldn't that derail the train?"

"Or make you float higher up, which actually would help old man Gordon here," he said. "Were you at Stonehenge? You look like someone I know."

"No," Gordon replied. "I'm sixteen."

"Not the time." My arms trembled and jaw clenched.

"Right, my bad, anyway, Agatha, I get it, this guy is a little weird," Imani said, "But the best thing about being a shield, even if you let someone in, they don't have to stay."

"What do you mean?"

"Have you ever been friends with someone, then they did you dirty and you never spoke to them again?"

"Yes," I replied, though it was few and far between because people suck and letting them in was hard.

"If Gordon here pisses you off, you can kick him out of the bubble, onto the train tracks and let his skull be crushed," Imani said, and I opened my eyes again. My eyebrows knitting together with the sick visual. "Even I couldn't save him if you did that."

"Really? We're doing this?" Gordon said.

"How many more of these are there?" Imani asked with a sardonic tone.

"Yeah, you can crush my skull, I guess," Gordon spat. "Actually, that might be exactly what I need."

He stepped forward, my heart clutched in my chest as I

feared him dropping to his death. Instead, he slipped through the shield and used the base to walk, extending the corridor as he did until he passed me.

Riley and Petra made fast work of welding the edges, and before I knew what happened Imani stepped through. Hopped a few times to test the weight, then placed his hands on my shoulders to lower my arms.

"That'll do pig."

"Did you just quote Babe?"

"What's Babe?" he teased with a wink.

Jerk.

"Come on, kid."

Turning me around I watched as Riley floated through to the next car and more people came out of the suites. Quickly understanding work needed to be done and moving through the newly attached corridor to help with the heavy lifting.

"You think you'll be able to do it again?" Imani asked, peering into an open suite and snagging an abandoned strawberry *Pop Tart* pack.

"Asking too much for you?" I questioned. My body weakened by the exertion and wanting to collapse.

"Communal living, right? What's yours is mine and what's mine is mine because I'm not officially a member of this little club yet."

"How is it all yours?" I asked.

"It's a mystery to me too," he replied. "That being said. How do you feel?"

"Exhausted."

He snapped one of the untoasted *Pop Tarts* in half and gave it to me. I wasn't a fan unless toasted with warmed butter melting into the strawberry goop in the middle. The addition was enough to soften the hard crust that was actually softer when cold ironically. This one had frosting, the strange no-no in our house. As if the frosting was the death knell of the so-called pastry. Honestly, the frosting made it better than I imagined. Or maybe it was the need for sugar.

Outside of the few grapes I'd popped while waiting, I don't remember the last time I ate. Peeking in the suite, I tried to figure out who it was. Without the spray-painted monikers we used as addresses, it was hard to know who I had to pay back.

"Each one will become easier," he said after a hard swallow of *Pop Tart*. "Fuel is necessary. At all times. Have you not noticed? You thought Riley was eating like crazy because he was a teenage boy?"

"I haven't really been paying attention to Riley eating." My eyes turned down, less disappointed than before about the loss of connection with my friend.

"Oh, shame, most *Amalgams* are nearly frail because of all the abilities burning in their system. He seems fit."

"Is that why you eat like you do?" I asked, nibbling a bit on the corner.

"Tracking you guys? Flying? Saving your life and then Gordon's. It takes a lot out of a guy."

"What you said to me, about letting people in my circle," I began.

"You don't," he replied. "I'm not sure why I'm a *flyer*. You say the *shifter* you have is a politician's son? Our gifts come from somewhere inside us. Were we born to our gifts? Or did they evolve to fit a need inside us?"

"Aggs," Riley called.

I stuffed the last of the pastry in my mouth. Holding my hand over my mouth, I spoke with a half full mouth. "If I can still move when this is done, we need to sit down and talk."

"Will there be pizza?" Imani questioned with a wink.

"Maybe."

"Well, there's your answer. Can you do this on your own yet?"

"No," I replied. The honesty a bit painful. Weakness, a

thing you were never supposed to admit, especially to strangers and Imani was far from an instant friend and confidant. Yet, here I was, being flown around and sweet-talked without a single shield in sight.

Learning to yield power had to have an easier route. A half dozen corridors sealed, at least at this point Imani could hang back. Searching out food like a starving man who, at some point, needed to fall into a food coma. I lost him when we hit a food car. Not that I was surprised. What did surprise me was him coming to find me after I'd been granted a second shower because I'd done so much work.

I took the blessing with gusto, for the simple reason every muscle in my body ached. Most of which I didn't know existed. Summer had disappeared and the last thing I want was Riley healing my aching muscles. Nope I was going old fashion with a warm shower, a few ibuprofens and my bed. Less than two minutes after I laid down, a knock on my door was followed by Imani letting himself in as if he were family.

Who was I to protest? I may have strained my pinkie toe if that was a real thing. Lord knows, my feet were cramping. Another thing I didn't know was possible. And here I thought laundry duty was hard. Standing still for five minutes at a time with my arms extended nearly killed me.

"Am I going to need to lift you up?"

"Why do I need to move?" I groaned into my pillow, having closed my eyes again and catching the faint whiff of garlic and red sauce. "Did you bring pizza?"

"No, sadly, I'm not really sure how you all do that here, but there was some lasagna being served and I explained why I needed a few pieces for the crew."

"And by crew you meant Riley, Petra and Gordon in addition to you and I."

"I've had a theory about reincarnation too," he said, not answering the question as my bed dipped when he sat setting off a round of muscle spasms. "You remind me of this girl I knew centuries ago."

"Devastatingly beautiful?" I joked.

"No, smart mouthed and in general highly skilled."

My torso floated upward, and I opened my eyes to see he was lifting me by my shirt and angling me to sit to the side.

"Fuel, you need fuel," he said, then reached into a backpack to retrieve a bottle. "And water. What is it with you all on here? These are the bare necessities of life, and you act as if they can be ignored."

Placing a pillow on my lap as a table, he set a container with the pasta in front of me then moved himself down on the bed and against the wall.

"Are you ever full?" I questioned, as he practically inhaled the first piece of lasagna.

"It's a chicken or egg thing, because honestly, once I start eating, it makes me hungrier."

"The world is your bag of chips?" I questioned as I cut a bite and pierced the layered pasta before bringing it to my mouth. Prepackaged and heated up, it warmed me none the less. Each drink of water flushed through my body, clearing out the lactic acid built up from all the exertion. I didn't want to admit it, but this did help.

"What you young ones need to understand, your powers are as much mental as they are physical. Even those you think are a hundred percent mental, they take a toll physically as well."

"Like Ms. Weston and her *whispering*."

His eyes cut to me, a strange look on his face as if he didn't know her power. Even though he'd said he knew her.

"What?"

"When I met her, she was known as a *bellwether*. Have you heard of the Pied Piper?" he questioned, popping the top on the second container of food. "That was Judith."

"Like a cult leader?" I questioned.

"For her day job, I guess. It wasn't like she'd been stiffed on a job clearing out rats though." This time he took his time cutting pieces off the lasagna before eating. "And children weren't her target. Leading men to their deaths, that's more what she was doing. Vince wasn't the only one in that family tree that had a nasty streak."

A chill shot down through my body. The little contact I'd had with Ms. Weston I have never thought of her as a cold-blooded killer. But if she could truly turn peoples mind, drive them insane by talking to them, what would be one step closer to killing them and making them take the step to avoid having the guilt of pulling the trigger.

"Whatever she's called now, that family has a past. A dark one," he said.

"But Riley," I reasoned, even if I now wasn't sure I could look at him the same after getting this information.

"I'm not sure how or when their bloodline went sour. But why is it their line fighting for supremacy?"

"Who said they were?" I questioned.

"Wasn't he the impertinent child that gave me his rank when I first met him?"

"Technically, yes, but he doesn't even like being the Vice President of this place," I stated.

"How would you know?"

His question hit harder than I expected in the center of my chest. How would I? Riley and I barely spoke anymore. Picking at my lasagna, I bit another piece to avoid answering the question.

"How is Ms. Weston the inspiration for the Pied Piper?" I

asked. Unsure if I should trust his word or what I've experienced from the Westons. People could change, couldn't they? Vince hadn't, but Riley had never given me pause. If anything, he was naïve to most things having been sheltered by the alleged monster.

"What do you know about lemmings?" he asked.

An hour later I stared at the wall across from me, unsure how to process hundreds of people walking off a high cliff and falling into the sea. Rocks splattered with blood one moment, only to be gone when the waves crashed against them. All started and processed by Riley's mother, who I overheard telling him to never trust anyone. Riley was the opposite. He stuck up for his friends. Trusted them without a fault. If there was any of the sickness in him, wouldn't our *Soul Reader* have seen the darkness? She saw me being caged off. I needed Claire to read Imani because I feared I was the one being taken in like a stooge.

Too much of what he's been saying contradicts the world I've come to know. Moreover, I didn't know why I wanted to believe him over my friends who I've come to trust. I rolled to the side and reached for my sneakers. Tugging them on my bare feet and not caring that I was in lounge pants and a cami because I foolishly thought I was going to sleep. Standing, I wobbled a bit. While my feet reminded me, the recharging was only step one.

"You okay? Do I need to get you a healer?" he asked, reaching out, his hand encircling my wrist.

"I'm good, but I need you to come with me."

Stepping out into the hallway, I came up short and stared. Cynthia must have been through because a tree, fully formed with honey crisp apples, was now in our hallway. The branches bent upward, with only a few hanging low. One side pressed firmly along the outer wall, and I wondered if she'd had an orchard where she lived. If so how big would this tree be? Now it was me being greedy and snagging two before moving backward on the train. Unease about walking through gone as I made my way, finding new treats along the way. When I turned back, I saw Imani filling his shirt with a veritable fruit basket.

"How far back are we going?" he asked. Crossing through bathrooms, showers, and the food stations.

The bustle of Satori was evident. With each railcar we opened, people breathed freer. The only spot the crew and I hadn't gone while installing corridors was the engine room. Having already been connected early on. A new project would be started. One I wasn't in the mood to learn about because I feared I'd be tapped. Who knew when or where we would stop the next time?

Approaching the last three cars, I slowed. It was late, but not having windows allowed us to make our own time. A few people lived by the clock, *Harveys* mostly, tasked to pay their way by working. The rest of us were left to our own schedule, what worked for us and our recovery. Something Imani and the elders are going to need to teach us.

"A locked door?" Imani questioned. "Am I being brought into the inner sanctum?"

His question made me uneasy. We'd been warned by Ms. Weston to make sure Vince never knew we had a *soul reader*. Only now I wasn't sure, having heard the tale of Ms. Weston leading people to their death, who to believe. A description so foreign to me it made my head hurt and stomach clench.

Flashbacks to sneaking downstairs to turn on the nightly news as they described my father in all his horrible glory. At first, I'd convinced myself they weren't talking about him. Or I was missing words because the volume was so low. Only reading things running along the bottom of the screen told the truth. The man had betrayed friends; ones who'd brought their kids to play with me were now in a destroyed home because of him. My father, my hero, had broken more than a promise to take me to school for my first day until I graduated.

Hurt caused acid to creep up my throat, and I nearly dropped my two apples. Turning to Imani, I shook my head, trying not to laugh at the distracted man with a plum in his mouth while arranging the other things he'd picked in his makeshift shirt basket.

"How long were you alone?" I asked.

"Are any of us every truly alone?" he replied, the ability to turn any question into a philosophical debate had me shaking my head. "What's behind the door? Dungeon? Torture chamber? Swimming pool?"

"Depends on the night," a disembodied voice came from a small speaker in the upper corner of the railcar behind a camera I hadn't noticed. "What's up Aggs? I thought you'd be sleeping."

"Hey Peyton, can I come in?"

"Just you?"

"Why, you want some fresh fruit?" I questioned, thumbing toward Imani.

"Possibly," Peyton replied. "I really haven't been able to wander and check out the new stuff."

"It's amazing, really," I replied. "I have a tree in my hallway lobby."

"Maybe she'll put one in my suite then I'll never have to leave."

"You would just be the wizard behind the triple locked door," I replied.

The sound of bolts moving made me take a step back as I held out the second apple I was carrying.

"There are six," Peyton corrected when the door was finally opened.

Dark circles hung heavy under his normally rested brown eyes. His hair was usually shaved bald, but today there was a slight growth of his stubbly black hair. I wondered if he'd have thick, spiral curls if he let his hair grow out or more of an afro.

Taking the apple I offered, he bit and leaned on the doorjamb. His eyes cut to the stranger behind me. Peyton's rank and importance meant he not only knew of every person in Satori, but he'd also done the research on them and made sure they were clear to live there. The few times I'd seen him when I returned after being rescued from Vince, he hadn't appeared much better. Maybe he blew through Vince's vetting too quickly or missed when he slipped in past our security. However, Vince got into our safety net and Peyton was taking it as a personal failure. One he should have seen coming from a myriad of reasons. Least of which his ability to predict things since he was a *seer*.

"How can I be of assistance?" he asked.

"I'm assuming someone is tucked away in your suite," I said.

"You make me sound like some pervert who kidnaps people."

"You're the one who admitted to having a dungeon in there," Imani said, and Peyton's eyes narrowed. "Sorry, that's rude, or my new best friend is rude. I'm Imani."

"Imani what?" Peyton questioned with a tone darker than I'd ever heard.

"What is it with you kids and surnames?" Imani shook his head a few times. "Deng. Imani Deng, yes I'm a bit over a thousand years old."

"Like sixteen, seventeen years," Peyton surmised.

"And they say common core math is making it hard on kids these days. Honestly, I've watched some of those videos. It seems like you're taking eleven extra steps. But you know how us people that have done things since the ancients invented the concept are stuck in our ways." He waved his hand in dismissal toward Peyton. "What can I say? Our way is obviously stupid."

"Okay, does he ever stop talking?" Peyton asked.

"I'd say when eating, but as you can tell, he got all that out while finishing a mixed green salad."

"Needs dressing," Imani replied, while crunching a carrot and coughing a bit. "That being said, your grower is amazing. This tastes familiar. Is Cindy here?"

"Carrots?" Peyton said, raising his eyebrow.

"Okay, those were weird because they hang from the ceiling," I explained.

"I really need to explore," Peyton said.

"No, you need to rest," the ethereal voice of Claire said as she opened the door wider.

Riley once questioned if she was an angel, and it was hard to not equate the two. Her platinum blonde hair shimmered, the pale skin barely pinked unless around someone who darkened her spirit. The strangest part was her eyes. The irises nearly devoid of color completely one minute, then a pale blue gray the next. Being a *soul reader* meant she also took on the darkness around her. Even if Peyton was drained, his heart had to be pure because she wasn't locked away with him due to her importance. The two were together. Now more than before, when she was tucked away in a suite at the edge of our compound. There was no escaping the others outside of staying with Peyton. Unlike Dina, who couldn't block out the voices, for Claire, being around too many people could make her physically ill.

While Riley had taken on her powers, much like all the rest of his powers, he was the jack of all trades, but master of none. The last thing he was thinking of when he saw Imani was to clear him. Not that I blame him. Most, especially elders, aren't willing to share. Or maybe they had been burned by an *amalgam* in the past. Either way, unlike Claire, it wasn't Riley's job to clear people.

Peyton encircled Claire's hand with his and stepped slightly in front of her. She closed her eyes for a moment, as if trying to settle herself after taking on a great burden. Imani's eyes widened a bit as a smirk came to his currently empty lips.

"Ah, I believe your charge is to be tasked to me," Imani said, causing Peyton's shoulders to stiffen and chest jut out.

"Imani's an elder—"

"We must come up with a better term," he interjected.

"Okay, ancient one." I paused, waiting for more than his groan, but this time he stayed silent. "He needs to be cleared."

"Yes, because saving your life twice and that wayward ginger wasn't enough to let you know I'm safe."

Crossing my arms, I turned. "You said some pretty unfavorable things about people we've come to trust."

"You trusted Vince," he countered. "Did she clear him?"

"No," Peyton said. "He wasn't an *aberration*, that we knew of, and from what I've been told she wouldn't have been able to see anything if she tried."

"He probably wouldn't have allowed it." Imani held a cucumber, the last thing from his shirt basket. "Any chance you have salt in there?"

"You're just going to eat that like you did the carrot?" I questioned.

"You've met me, right?" he shook his head. "It's only been a few hours, but seriously I thought we had a connection."

Claire slipped from behind Peyton into the entryway and stared up at Imani.

"Hello sweetness," he purred.

Instantly, my hand flew to Peyton's chest to stop him from snapping. Between exhaustion, their relationship and his natural want to protect, he was on edge.

"You have a rare gem on this little rolling circus," Imani said as Claire passed me the cucumber and took Imani's hands. "A millennium of living and never have I met one like you. Heard the stories, know the signs, but never had the pleasure."

"Can you pass me that cucumber?" Peyton asked. "I might want to shove it somewhere."

"Careful," Imani replied. "I wouldn't want your girl to think you're flirting with me."

Claire's face gave no indication about what she was seeing, though her hair didn't darken. Summer spoke of Claire having jet black hair when she first arrived. The poison of the world weighing down on her with a mix of ailments. Now eliminated, and not only by Summer's healing touch. Dangerous people had brought the dark colors, between the limited contact with others and Peyton's good heart she stayed clear. The darker her hair turns, the blacker the soul. That was the outward display of what the person was about, but what she was deeper. Into their heart, the truth and lies couldn't be hidden from her. She'd created a scale of who and what was dangerous. Colors flowed through the center of every person, much like an aura, but deeper. She saw my shield. Transparent, but strong like a crystal enclosing my heart.

"Scars, I assume all your age have some," Claire said. "And still…"

"I'm devastatingly handsome." Imani winked at me. "I know a blessing and a curse," he said with a bit of lift to his voice. "You understand that don't you, you little minx."

"Yeah, I'm gonna need that cucumber," Peyton growled.

"Down," Claire said with a light smile, then stroked Imani's cheek. "He's harmless. Scars made without a blade. Under the skin and brought about by living. That is all that mar his heart. Now these inconsistencies, who were they about?"

"Riley's mother," I said. "Vince isn't the only one with a dark past."

"Then come in," Claire said, holding the door wide. "And we'll shine light on it."

CHAPTER EIGHT

One thing I've learned is wounds don't heal when you keep picking at them. Each time we thought we were healing, life was settling, and we believed in the future again, another bombshell would drop. A year after we were born, towers fell, and our country went on red alert. By our fifth birthday, New Orleans was slammed with what we were told was a once in a lifetime storm. Only our life had now seen so many since then they stopped saying that. When we started school, active shooting drills were as commonplace as fire and tornado drills.

Then we hit puberty. Mutations appeared, and we became the number one enemy on the planet. Locking down, being shipped off for our safety and that of the country—world, really. Across the planet, the year two thousand no longer meant a new beginning, it was when the dangerous ones were born.

"We need to hold a tribunal," Peyton said as we sat in the area set up as his meeting area.

The council no longer consisted of all the *aberrations*. Only those higher up, chosen by Trent, make the real decisions. With Riley being his second. And here we were, about to pull a three-thousand-year-old lawyer, with the ability to whisper, to explain herself in front of a group of us. Including her son.

"That's your decision. I only came to see if we needed to toss him." I thumbed to Imani, who held his hand splayed on his chest in mock hurt.

"You need to be on the panel," Peyton said.

"The hell I do." I stood and headed to the door. "I'm not going anywhere near something that might send Ms. Weston off the train."

"We all know you like Riley—"

"I swear if I hear that one more time, I'm going to rip the person's voice box out," I snarled.

"But that's not your skill," Imani said.

"Isn't it?" I challenged, trying my best to hold my evilest glare. "You don't know me."

"True, but I'm enjoying learning about you." He waved his hand to the spot next to him. "Now come, sit."

Why I did as I was told proved I was exhausted and subject to inducement. With a hard sigh, I plopped. Sure, I'd been awake for at least a full day and at this point I was slowly slipping into hysteria. The room began to swim around me. My eyes cut to Imani, who was holding a conversation I couldn't hear with Peyton and Claire. I tried to push up against the couch, but I might as well be covered with a weighted blanket. One hammered to the floor, trapping me. Overheated, I couldn't figure out if I'd been drugged. Would Peyton or Claire protect me? Would they even notice?

I struggled, muscles burning as if the hold on me were magnetic and stuck on all my joints. Imani glanced over his shoulder, his eyes smiling as he raised his finger and placed it in the middle of my forehead.

"You need sleep," he said, the words hitting me once again like a command I couldn't deny. The moment the P in sleep hit my ears, the world went dark, and I was lost in a dream.

Boys had a smell, not always bad if they showered and used cologne. While Summer, Claire or I were usually floral, Riley, Petra or in the case of this pillow, the boy was spice. Some part dark, others fresh. Peyton must be the owner of the bed I woke up in because it was a king size in a room with two dressers. The most important part was it wasn't my bed.

Lifting the covers, I was happy to see my jammies in place. Only my sneakers had been removed. Had Imani really knocked me out with a word? Or a suggestion? What was going on? Pulling back the covers, I rolled to the side and sat up. No major vertigo was a bonus from where I had been—I couldn't say hours ago, for all I know I had a fifteen-minute power nap. Slipping on my sneakers, I stood and wandered to the opening where I assume I'd been before I passed out.

Voices were low, but it seemed as if there were more than the three people I'd abandoned when exhaustion overtook me. At least I hope it was exhaustion and nothing to do with Imani.

"It is time," Claire said once I stepped into view.

"How long?" I asked, thumbing toward the bedroom.

"Long enough," Imani said, and I narrowed my eyes at him.

"We're almost to the California border," Peyton explained. "Summer is coming back in a few minutes."

"He was getting worried," Imani explained. "As if I'd hurt my best friend."

"And that would be?" I questioned, spinning my hand as if that would pull the real answer out of him.

"You silly. I shared not only grapes, but lasagna with you," he scoffed. "Is there any bigger show of undying devotion than sharing pasta?"

Claire gave me a shrug, her hair pulled back in a loose

French braid. The silvery strands framing her face, catching any stray light in the room. She was sitting with her legs tucked underneath her in an oversized recliner. Or her slight frame made it appear larger than needed. I was torn between wanting her to tell me Imani was dangerous and assuring me he was safe. Maybe it was because I wanted to believe in something more but feared my reality. What had Claire said about scars deeper than the skin? Brought on by living.

"Are you sure he's safe?" I questioned.

"He has taught me something," Peyton said. "He's not only a *flyer*, he's a *pusher*."

"I thought only one person could be an *amalgam*." Taking a step back, finding the sliver of hope we could live without one of the bigger threats. "If he's alive, then Riley doesn't need to be sacrificed. You said you were one of Vince's prisoners. He knows this. Why is he trying to kill Riley?"

"He's a *duelist*," Peyton said.

"A what?"

"You ask if you can trust him. No clue, but he has more than one ability." Peyton shook his head and shrugged. "Elders know things, but not everything. Not by a long shot. Trust him or don't. We don't know."

"What can we say, when we gathered in groups, people like Vince happened." Imani opened a bag of chips. "At times we passed information along, but you guys have better records. Well, better than most."

"What about Rodem?" I asked, and Imani nearly choked on a mouthful of chips.

Peyton reached over and slapped his back to clear the airway. Imani held his hand up after a few hard slaps.

"You guys know about Rodem? How do you already know —you know what? Maybe we'll actually figure out what we really are. That is if the *Harveys* don't kill us first."

"*Harveys* are only unblessed born in the year two thousand."

"Do you have a vocab list? I feel like the old guy that doesn't understand the lingo. I hate that." Imani shook his bag of chips around before plucking a perfect whole chip from the bag.

"You haven't earned the right to see our research," Peyton said, holding up a finger. "But you can help us add to it."

"Always the bridesmaid." Imani returned to eating his bag of chips.

"We need to stop feeding him," I said.

"Rude." Imani's eyebrows knitted together.

A screen attached to the wall by the door lit up, obviously triggered by motion, and we could hear those outside the door clearly.

"Fixing those corridors wasn't easy," Riley said. "Her passing out isn't a stretch."

"According to Peyton, the guy has powers like yours," Trent said. Their voices slightly crackled over the speaker by the door. "No, like more than one."

Ms. Weston appeared exhausted or exasperated. Either way, the hard sigh as she stepped behind her son was audible through the room. Peyton pressed a button, and the sound of the door unlocking had all three visitors shift their attention to the doorway.

"Take the food from him," Ms. Weston ordered once she'd stepped into the room, and Imani clutched the bag of chips to his chest.

The sound of the bag being smooshed echoed through the railcar. No words were spoken between those inside. I was trying to understand Ms. Weston's command. She'd never ordered anyone or anything before. Even Riley seemed a bit put off by his mother's gruff tone. The ease and peace I'd actually discovered for a half a second vanished as the tips of

Claire's hair reddened as if they'd been dipped in a can of paint.

"I know what you're doing, Imani." Ms. Weston held her hand out, with hopes violence wouldn't be needed to remove the snack from his clutches.

Imani's jaw moved, chewing the last of what was in his mouth before swallowing. Savoring in a way, the last bit of nourishment allowed him.

"Let me guess, he's been eating us out of house and train since he arrived?" Ms. Weston's lips pursed in disapproval.

"Rude," Imani scoffed while rolling the bag of chips down to seal it.

"Pretty much," I confessed.

"Did the pasta mean nothing to you?" he questioned, his voice an octave higher than normal and eyes batting at me.

"He's preparing for a hiberfast," Ms. Weston stated, as if that cleared anything up.

"Wrong." Imani unrolled the bag to resume eating as he clearly explained. "I'm coming out of a hiberfast."

"Sure you are, we all know—"

"Don't be saying that. I had a legitimate reason that time."

"Define legitimate," Ms. Weston countered.

The conversation twisted and turned between the two, with enough shared history to leave out key details. Riley's head pivoted on a swivel between the volleying barbs. Imani and Ms. Weston argued like a pair of siblings over the last brownie. Only I didn't know who to cheer for. Was this how it was to be Riley? Trying to figure out a world constantly spinning sideways.

"What is hiberfasting?" Peyton snatched the chips bag and tossed them across the room.

"Okay, this will be my third rude, in less than ten minutes. Honestly, has no one taught you all manners?"

"It's a trick Vince tortured out of Rodem," Ms. Weston said.

And finally, a point goes to one of the players in the sick game of trust. Any explanation had to have worth. Information at this point had to be teased out of the elders like a teacher wanting us to do our own research without even giving us the courtesy of passing us so much as a textbook to pull from.

"Vince?" Riley and Trent both straightened their shoulders like synchronized swimmers. The President and Vice President of the makeshift rolling country agreed on one major point of fact. Anything surrounding that name required a deep dive to find the truth.

"Don't look at me like that. I was his—"

"Victim? Stooge? Or lacky?" Trent asked, his eyes bore into Imani to the point even I wanted to protect the poor guy.

"Guinea pig or lab rat. You tell me, shifter. Which animal gets the most torture?"

"And yet." Ms. Weston crossed her arms.

"Just because a sociopath has an idea, doesn't make it bad," Imani reasoned.

"I believe it's a red flag," Trent replied.

"Still. Not always bad." Imani raised a finger. "And can have good outcomes."

"Name one," Riley snapped.

"I missed most of the *Celali Rebellion*." Imani stretched his arms high.

"Explain," I finally snapped. My brain wanting to explode. By now I should be used to the new realities hitting at eighty miles per hour, but everyone has a breaking point and mine just slammed me right between the eyes. Rolling up into a ball and hiding in the corner wasn't currently on the table for me, so explosion was my only option.

"The what?" Peyton asked.

"It was a mix of uprisings and small wars that lasted about a hundred and fifty years in parts of the Ottoman Empire," Ms. Weston said flippantly, as if we should have learned of it during elementary school. "You know we missed you then."

"Still not explaining," I spat, the irritation inching up my spine and shooting down my arms. My fingers splayed wide, then fisted over and over.

"Think Thanksgiving," Ms. Weston said. "Much like a bear, we can eat our way into unconsciousness."

"We can get the 'itis' for a hundred and fifty years?" Peyton questioned.

"I've never gone past about seventy-five," Imani stated. "But checking out is healthy. Just make sure you find a good place to hide when you do it. The last thing you want to do is wake up to a man with a shovel, or worse a wooden box."

The whole vampire legend surrounding Vince was on full display and my whole body had to do the stupid shiver and jerk. Riley's eyebrows knitted together in worry, and I waved him off. Not wanting to acknowledge what I'd just done. Why was Ms. Weston so worried Imani was going back into a hiberfast? She and Imani weren't ready to kill each other. In fact, they were pretty cordial. How long did it take to knock oneself into a hiberfast? Right now, I was ready to gorge myself into oblivion because nothing, and I mean nothing, made me want to stay in the room where I was currently trapped.

CHAPTER NINE

"Mom, how long have you known him?" Riley asked after we'd finally got the breakdown of hiberfasting with Imani and Ms. Weston, debating the pros and cons of it all.

Sure, there was a chance you'd be buried, but until embalming became popular, you were only in danger if you passed out in an area that believed in setting the dead ablaze. Being burned on a pyre wasn't a good Saturday, Imani warned. And much like it was now, you couldn't really ask for another *aberration* to watch over you. Only, I would trust Riley to watch over me for a long-needed nap. Summer too. Claire or Peyton even. Maybe we were naïve, but the few conversations I'd been able to have with Riley let me know he'd rather trust and be wrong than never trust anyone.

Had that been why I'd fallen so quickly for Imani, pulling him into the fold and not totally trying to lock him away? He'd saved my life, or at least rescued me from being left behind. Gordon did owe him his life, and I would never have been able help Riley connect the moving train without Imani pushing me because Riley did his best to never use his own power of persuasion on me. The scales of justice in my head

114

weren't so much trying to find balance as they were trying to not have the beam at the top snap from too much overall weight. The largest and heaviest of all being the bombshell shared about Ms. Weston.

"We met when Vince's castle had been raided," Ms. Weston said, shaking the scales free of all pieces of information so I could begin reweighing them.

It was the way she spoke. The way a mother would her newborn, reverent and fearful of making a mistake. Wanting to comfort and yet knowing in a few years she would be tossed aside for a school friend.

"Cynthia was still healing or trying to heal the best she could. I'd gone into the castle in search of survivors with a few others who'd helped us send Vince away." Ms. Weston shook her head. "Honestly, we were trying to quell any supporters."

"You didn't know about the people he was torturing?" Peyton asked.

"We did," she confessed. "But we assumed he and his lackies had killed them on their way out of the fortress. No witnesses, no trial."

For the first time, Imani set food aside. Placing both feet on the ground, he leaned forward, his forearms resting on his knees as his hands came together as if in prayer. Releasing all the air in his lungs his eyes met Ms. Weston's for a moment until they had to both turn their focus away.

"The levels of dungeons had to have been inspired by Dante," Ms. Weston said.

"Or the writer had survived the initial rounds," Imani said. "We'll never know what came first. The chicken or the torture chamber."

"I'm not sure—" I shook my head, unaware of all the levels of torture Dante had written about, to me it was general knowledge that Dante had come back from Hell and wrote what he'd seen down in an epic poem. Either way changing torture chamber to egg wasn't exactly the best way to get at the truth. "Sorry."

"Those of us fighting against Vincent gathered the survivors, and each chose some to help." Ms. Weston pulled in on her lips. "In a way, Imani and Cynthia healed each other more than I did. The distraction of helping someone else blocked their own suffering."

"My mother saved you and you accuse her of atrocities," Riley said.

"That's why I'm here?" Ms. Weston questioned. "I thought you wanted to know about Imani."

"Six of one, half dozen of the other," Trent stated. "He accused you and well, if you think we don't trust our own parents, we aren't exactly ready to forgive the elders that let us flounder for years."

"You weren't the only ones scared. Trust me when I say your generation is different for so many reasons," Ms. Weston said. "But we do know what happens to those who are gifted."

"That and you were never part of our plan," Peyton said as Claire slipped in behind him and locked her hand with his.

How much had Peyton seen of our future? This is why I didn't want to be part of the council. Ducking my head and pushing through was my baseline. Knowledge was power, and I have been happy to stay powerless. A cog in the system helping it run with little to no understanding of what the machine was producing. Stuffed bears? Nuclear missiles? As long as my bed was clean and food was hot, I was good.

"How much of the plan has come true?" Imani asked. "*Seers* fascinate me, the real, imagined, can you duck it or not?"

"Enough," Peyton said.

"And there wasn't a dark shadow lurking?" Imani questioned, throwing out an image of himself. "Good aura, dark soul and a conundrum for sure."

Peyton's jaw tightened and Claire moved her other hand to his bicep. Her hair shifting like a mood ring trying to settle in on the color, telling me I wasn't the only conflicted person in the room.

"What did you tell them?" Ms. Weston asked.

"The truth," Imani replied. "Though who was I to know they would go all judge and jury on my ass afterward."

"What is he talking about, Mom?" Riley asked.

"When we cleared the castle, I'd seen things," she said and the whole room chilled. "Things those he'd left behind found acceptable. As if what they had done was for the greater good. Worse were the ones who would be unable to unlive what they'd experienced. There was no therapy then. Good and evil in all its varying degrees. That was all we knew. Even that was up for interpretation."

"The dark ages they say," Imani's voice was hushed. "Only darkness was in men's souls then."

"Vince's castle was on a high cliff." Ms. Weston rubbed her upper arms and then closed her eyes for a moment. "Letting someone go can be as charitable as saving them."

She crossed the space between Imani and herself, her hand cupping his cheek for a moment, before running her finger over the scarred upper lip of the old friend.

"I can only suggest, lead others with thoughts already racing in their heads." She turned to face us. "Not all were gifted and while it is hard to kill us, it is not impossible. You saw that firsthand when we rescued Riley and Aggie."

"You slaughtered them?" Trent asked.

"No, but I delved into their minds. Whispering the thoughts that would haunt them at night. Only louder, and more pronounced. They were fresh from the bloodbath. Bodies worked, but minds were numb. It was as if I were wading through waist high oatmeal."

"You never pushed a jury to convict when you were a

lawyer," Riley said, trying to equate two realities that were worlds apart. "You only called on their better virtues, but you never told me what would happen if they didn't have them?"

"Bet you wanted a hiberfast after dealing with them," Imani said. "We barely made it back to your home."

"What did she do?" Claire finally spoke even though it was clear.

Ms. Weston's azure eyes became dark as eggplant without the ability to capture light on the rubbery skin. "I reminded them." Her voice hoarse as the memory clawed its way up her throat. Viscous and unwilling to stay bottled up inside but making sure it would leave a painful wound when reopened. "Reminded and questioned them of how a person could stand by and watch. My mind unable to shake the vision of blood and guts. The screams from those disemboweled, but alive until one of us had to cut their throat to stop the screams of anguish."

"Gut wounds don't kill like they do in the movies. Quick, with a few coughs of blood." Imani brought his hands, still in prayer to his lips. "They fester, for days, even weeks. The smell of rot and excrement bringing out the creatures that live on that. A circle of life played out on a scale unimagined as the person passes out from pain only to be awakened by sickness to find vermin eating them alive."

Claire buried her face against Peyton's shoulder, and I wished there was some way I too, could escape. Could my shield be used to block the words? Turn them into muffled noises on the other side of a wall?

"I reminded them," Ms. Weston explained. "Of humanity, and those they'd harmed. Others, I gave them an out. A way to make it all go away because when I looked in their eyes, I saw they had lost more than a limb or their dignity."

"You went too far," Imani said. "Even you admitted to that."

"I didn't send you," she replied apologetically. "Not on purpose."

"Thank goodness for Mei or I would have been sent headfirst off the edge without even thinking about flying."

"I said I was sorry," Ms. Weston said, her lips pulling in tightly. "That why you're trying to get me tossed from here?"

"No," he replied. "What I see is a group gathering and from what I heard Vince had already made his way inside."

Ms. Weston nodded her head in agreement and sighed a bit. "I've tried to warn them, but the ignorance of youth has them believing this generation is different."

Riley stood defiant and proud, shoulders broad. The flop of hair he rarely combed pulled back from his eyes for once by a ballcap.

"My son's the worst. You'd think I would have raised him better," she said. "How long were you out?"

"About twenty-five years give or take," Imani said as the old friends fell back into a routine of catching up and not acknowledging the bomb they had dropped.

"I envy you," Ms. Weston said, then turned to Riley. "But then again, I had quite a few blessings while awake."

"So, what?" Trent said. "We're just good then? No biggies, best friends for life now?"

"You know I did see this movie when I woke up where they talked about thunder buddies," Imani said, and Ms. Weston held out her hand as if to silence him as laughter overtook her.

"What just happened?" I asked, more so I could see if I could leave than actually caring about the current stance of either elder.

An alarm bell sounded from behind us. The railcar connected to Peyton's private suite sending a warning. Peyton swiftly moved past us, back through the hall. Trent and Riley in lockstep behind him as my skin rose and a sharp inhale of breath got stuck in my throat.

"I'm assuming that's important," Imani said.

"Probably," Ms. Weston replied, and made her own way back through the car.

"Aren't you joining?" Imani asked as I inched my way closer to the opposite door.

"Don't force me," I replied, the pleading evident in my words.

"Has Riley ever been able to use his power to persuade on you?" Imani questioned.

"No." I rubbed my upper arms to try to dissipate the cold. "Maybe, if so I didn't notice."

"I hate to tell you this, at some point, like it or not, you're going to have to become a bigger part of this."

Claire stepped to me, and her hand stroked along my cheek and her eyes widened.

"A door," she stated simply. "Your wall has a door now. Imani can go in."

"What about Riley? Or you?" I questioned. Why this stranger I'd known for a blip of time and not my friends? The people I'd allowed myself to believe and trust, at least I thought I had.

"Not yet," she said, the silvery strands finally setting and staying one color. "But we will need you too."

Claire pushed up on tipped toes and kissed my forehead as if she were a grandmother and not the one who saw into our souls. Our true selves. Even I was unable to block the probe she sent out.

Riley rushed from the second railcar, with Trent and Peyton not far behind. His mother stood in the doorway as if I'd put a shield up to block her. Her face ashen and body visibly trembling.

"If you ever cared for my son, go with him," she pleaded from the doorway.

My mind swirled, twisting end over end when I realized she was speaking directly to me. Not Trent or Imani, who had both offensive and defensive powers. Me. The one who summoned her power on accident or when pushed and then had little to no control over it.

Riley caught my hand and pulled me from the room. "We found Taylor."

CHAPTER TEN

Over the years, you're raised knowing what and who was a hero. Firemen ran into burning buildings as others were running out. Navy SEALs went into battle with full understanding they may never come home again, but it was for a good cause. Even in sports, we'd see the people that would leave it all on a field or court for the chance at immortality. Bringing the victory to those who were willing to go into the trenches with them. A bond, brought on between these groups by sweat, hard work and occasionally blood.

None of which appealed to me.

My heart was thudding, my stomach twisting, and I was pretty sure I'd lost most of my sight in my left eye from the searing migraine stabbing me through my eyeball. Riley's hand was the only connection I had to the real world. I wasn't even sure if my feet were actually moving. Maybe I was floating through the corridors, or he it was like a cartoon where the person in front was running so fast the other was basically a flag behind them. Everything was a blur and the wish I had to block out the story the elders spoke of now was in place. Whatever Riley said after the word, Taylor was lost in a tunnel, distant and being washed over by the sea. All of it in my ear in a way I'm sure Dina would appreciate. Muffled, unintelligible, and blocked completely from my brain.

Nodding would say I was in agreement about what was happening, but I hadn't done that. I'd done nothing but stare blankly ahead as I was being pulled cartoon style through the corridors. My wrist burned where Riley had a firm grasp and if anything could save me, it was the pain helping me register I was a conscious being.

I didn't know how far down the train we were going or why I was needed. The wind whipped past me, generated by Riley's speed when he could have just leaped where he wanted to go. Instead, I wondered if he'd found someone with hyper speed to leech off of. Fur began floating in the air around me, causing me to cough, and I saw Trent's body morphing before me. The black of his shirt and pants helping him become a slick panther. I wondered if he would have chosen a leopard or jaguar if he'd been wearing different clothing. No matter the shift had people jumping back and out of the way as we crossed through spaces, dodging plants created by Aunt Cindy.

Trent must have had to fight feline urges as he bound by the apple tree outside my suite. He'd rebounded off the wood as if he were ready to climb it, only to reverse course and let go with a sharp roar.

Personally, I believe I forgot to breathe. Holding my breath for eighty plus cars wasn't actually possible. Forgetting the basics of life, more reasonable. The hard inhale when we finally stopped outside of a similarly locked railcar like Peyton's had me gasping. Small sips of air making it into my lungs as Riley bent at the waist for a moment before interlocking his fingers behind his head and standing like some track star.

Stars pin-pricked the vision I did have in my right eye. The left was still blown in a mass of fuzzy, frosted over glass way. I had a door now. Much like the train, I had the ability to open up and share my gift. Here I was, trying to calm my thundering heart, and more importantly, catch up to the discussion I hadn't been a part of.

"Taylor," I gasped as Riley pounded on the locked door. "We're—rushing—why—?"

"You a little out of shape Aggs?" Peyton asked, helping me steady myself since Riley had let me go.

"If—I—could—breathe, I'd hit you."

"Don't need you to breathe," Peyton said. "We're gonna be doing a run and scoop with a little help from your shield."

His fingers outlined a square in the air as wind rushed around me in a whirlwind. The guy had no idea how much phrases, including the words run and scoop, were on my butt kicking list.

"I'm not some puppet you can just command," I said. "I can't even command me."

"And yet, here we are," Imani said, having come in from outside. "Sorry, running is so taxing on a person. Judith said I might be useful."

"Why? Why are you all doing this to me?" I cried, my fingers digging into my hair as I dropped to a crouched position.

"Because she'd do it for you," Riley reasoned. "If you'd been the one he'd kidnapped, wouldn't you have held out hope we'd rescue you?"

When did blind compassion turn into willful ignorance? Riley was pretty damn close to both right now and I didn't have the energy or will to fight him. I was in my dang jammies. Riley stripped off his hoodie and passed it to me. Giving me the shirt off his back, as if that wasn't who he was all the time. At some point, a halo was going to glow above his head.

"We help each other," he said as I pulled the hoodie, warm from Riley's body heat, over my head and was hit with the fresh scent of soap. "From the start you've been looking out for me."

Riley helped pull my hair from inside the sweatshirt, his hand lingering a bit on the back of my neck as he pulled me to his chest. My fingers curled in the T-shirt he wore before my arms wrapped around him, and I finally accepted his hug. At least a foot taller than me, my face was buried in his chest and his chin rested on the top of my head. Squeezing tight, I may have held on longer than I should, but couldn't help it. My shield wasn't out, but there was a bubble around me, and I felt safe.

The door opened and Riley released me, stroking my back to let me know it would be okay. Jessa, part of the protective detail, stood steadfast. In black pants, long sleeve T-shirt and what could only be described as a bulletproof vest. Her eyes narrowed, then cut down to Trent, still in panther form.

"I was hoping it was a drill," she said, removing a binder from her wrist and pulling back her long brown hair before twisting it into a bun. "Anyone want to lie to me and say it is?"

"Oh, dear child, lies just lead to anger when the truth comes out," Imani said. "Playing war never prepares one for the real thing."

"Who's the old man oracle?" Jessa asked.

"Suddenly elder isn't a bad word," he replied.

"Imani, Jessa," Riley introduced the two. "Jessa, Imani, he showed up after the attack."

"This is great and all," Trent said, then coughed with a bit of gagging afterward, having shifted back to human form.

"Hairball?" Imani questioned with a raised eyebrow. "You had time to lick yourself?"

"Did we decide if we were going to kick him out?" Trent asked, then waved his hands in the air as if to clean the air and get back on track. "No time, we're less than three minutes from where we need to jump."

"Jump?" I questioned, hands out in a hard stop. "Why are we jumping? And who is this we you speak of? Am I part of the we? I know I'm not part of we!"

"Do you know how long it takes to stop a train?" Peyton questioned. "Especially at our current speed and with as many cars as we have? Miles, Aggie, it would take miles and we'd overshoot our spot."

I held my hands, palm side up, creating a new set of scales to judge the updated information with. "Have to walk a few miles back to where Taylor is or jump off a train going over sixty miles per hour in what appears to be a wooded area?" I pointed to the still open sliding door left by Imani, where trees were zipping past us at a good clip. "I don't know Peyton, being one with a tree to me, never appealed to me. Especially when it involves me splattering on bark. And I'm assuming since you're not telling me I'm not part of the we you speak of, you expect me to jump from a moving train."

"You do better when you don't think," Imani said.

I stared, fish mouthed at him, my mind blanking completely.

"Good, Agatha is ready," Imani said as Petra, Gordon and Summer appeared, and Jessa began tossing backpacks toward us.

Numbly the straps were placed on my back as if I were half asleep and was being ushered onto a school bus. Summer held my shoulders and turned me away from the discussion going on behind me.

"Hey, Aggs, what's going on?"

"Why am I here?" I questioned, though I honestly couldn't tell even myself if I meant in this railcar, on the train, or on the planet. My breath was catching in my throat. Gulps of air choked me instead of filling my lungs. At least Summer had pulled my migraine away and I could see clearly, or maybe Riley had when he hugged me. Sadly, all I wanted to do was slam my eyelids shut and block the world where everyone else seemed to understand what they were here for.

"Hey, none of that," Summer said, pulling her own backpack on her shoulders and tying back her long blonde hair.

"Forty-five seconds," Peyton said.

My body was moved, because I know there was no way I would have placed myself at the side entrance to the railcar. Manmade wind from the speeding locomotive slammed into my face, my arms were gripped on either side of me as if a vice had been tightened to them. If I fell forward, to the blur of green and gray below, I would thud. No arms would break, at least from the impact. There was no bracing oneself. No. It was a freefall with my whole body breaking at once.

Hands were all around me. Like in *The Labyrinth* when Sarah fell down the hole. Only no faces were being made by spare hands. Pressure was building along my spine, muscle tightening like a twisted wet rag. Robbing me of valuable hydration. A countdown began. Struggling against the holds pressing my arms to my sides, weakness overtook me for a moment until Imani whispered louder than the wind.

"Protect us."

The words swished, swirled, and slammed into my heart. Crashing into the center of my chest with twisted tendrils around the rapidly beating organ. Air rushed from my lungs, my arms freed from their hold, sprang out from my sides. When I tumbled forward the bubble returned. The shield kept me hovering midair as the train zoomed behind me. Rumble from steel wheels on tracks told a story of my home, leaving me before quieting and then disappearing all together.

No one spoke, their hands warm where they stayed connected to me. The shove off the train jarring, but nothing compared to the variety of hands touching me. If Summer had clung to my back like a baby animal, my mind could process the connection. But hands? Various sizes randomly covering my shoulder, back, neck. All behind me like nightmares come to life if I turned to see them. Disembodied in a way, because distinguishing Summer from Jessa or Riley from Peyton was next to impossible. Had Trent shifted or was he the one on my hip? Had others from the protection detail joined in?

Imani descended, arms out, only missing a pair of massive wings to create the perfect angelic image. The smirk is what made my eye tick and when he reached out, touching the edge of my shield, it vanished, and I finally dropped to the ground with a thud. Behind me groans and dang its rang out.

"Warn a guy," Petra said, and I turned to see him standing but rubbing his hip. "By the way, the whole *Wizard of Oz* Good Witch bubble is pretty damn cool, Aggs."

"Who pushed me?" I snapped, after turning to face those who cajoled me into protecting them. "Who? You can't force—"

"Aren't we supposed to be rescuing your friend?" Imani questioned, cutting me off as if I had no right to stand up for myself.

"Seriously? I'm just supposed to forget I was tossed from a speeding train?"

Imani took my face in his hands. Warmth washed along my spine and my anger trickled away like a melting stream in springtime. Dualist my booty, this man had to be an *amalgam* like Riley, which meant Riley didn't need to die. Why else would his touch calm and soothe me the way Claire could.

"They wouldn't have tossed you if we didn't know you could protect yourself," he stated, his words metered and calm. "What you need to focus on is how to protect people you want to protect without having them touch you."

"I told you—" The words caught in my throat, tears of frustration fought to fall, but pride held them back. How could I express my lack of wanting to help in front of dozens of eyes, all of whom had rushed the moment we got word about Taylor? This wasn't about me. It never had been, and that was what Riley had been preaching to his mother.

Our generation, our group, was different from those in the past. We'd been through things the others hadn't. Known and seen things; connected to each other immediately. We didn't have to wander and hear stories hoping to find others like us. Thinking back to the attack. Had it been a day? Two? Time was a construct I couldn't grasp at the moment. No matter how far in the past when I thought about who attacked us, the only young one was Taylor.

She was a prisoner. One who may already have scars filled with Vince's blood, so they never truly heal. The pads of my fingertips traced along the scar marring Imani's face, rough, uneven edges and swollen in the middle. Jagged to add to the disfigurement. My own face still cradled in his hands, rough, but not calloused. Removing one from my cheek, I turned his hand palm side up and saw the burned flesh. Healed, but scarred over. Webbing a bit between his long fingers where a *healer* must have tried to graph skin. The bumps created a roadmap of pain.

"If Vince dies, does this go away?" I asked. "I mean, can it be healed?"

"That's the rumor, but that is not why I came with you to rescue your friend."

"Then why?" I asked, a tremble threatening to expose the troubling truth of my fears.

"Because you haven't fully learned to control your powers," he stated plainly. "And for some sick twisted reason, Little One, you allow me to bring it out of you."

"You're here for me?" I replied, swallowing back a mass of confused feelings.

Imani's other hand hadn't stopped cradling my face. His thumb brushed along my cheekbone sending a chill down my back. My stomach tightened and twisted while other parts of me warmed.

"Everyone else is here for your friend," he said. "Even you, whether you admit it or not, you are. Someone needs to be here for you."

I stepped closer, placing my hand on his stomach to stop myself from pressing into his body while still finding a connection. Every part of me wanted to be held and protected. My whole life, I had to put up a shield around myself. As much as I wanted to delude myself into believing my father had done what he'd done to make my life better, it was a lie. The money bought us a nice home and put me in private school, but he'd bought himself toys. Showed me off as if I were his pride and joy when in reality if he'd been looking out and protecting me, he never would have grifted those people. The large arms only gave me hugs to show others he was a good family man, a con so deep even I'd fallen for it.

Nannies were paid for; any affection shown contingent on a paycheck and disappeared the moment my normally absent mother no longer could pay them. There was no sweet story about a nanny still sending birthday wishes or Christmas greetings in my past. Even Summer brought me to Satori for her, not me, and deep in my soul I knew the truth.

"Why you?" I asked.

"There is little I know to be fact in the world, but one thing I do know, your heart knows good from evil. You just need to let your brain trust it." Imani bent down and kissed my forehead. "Little One, don't let the fear cloud your mind. Have you never been uncomfortable with a person an adult said was okay? Same thing, only backwards."

"I shouldn't trust you."

Imani wrapped his arms around me and pulled me flush to his chest, my arms holding tight to him as he cradled my head. "And yet, here we are."

CHAPTER ELEVEN

"What was that?" Summer said as she rushed to be by my side when we'd started to make our way through the thick forest of Northern California.

"What was what?" I asked. The world was sideways and for the most part all I could do was try to not trip.

"The thing with you and the old guy."

"Imani?" I questioned, though it was clear as the only elder among the group of us who she was talking about.

"I'm sorry, is there another thousand-year-old man around?" Summer nudged me with her shoulder, and I had to stick my arm out and push against a tree to right myself. "You like an old dude."

"He's been helping me learn to manage my shield."

"He's trying to date you and here I thought Riley was your man," she said.

"Not everyone is trying to be coupled up."

"If you were, who would you choose?" she asked, and I glanced over my shoulder to see Riley walking between two of the protection council members.

No wonder I couldn't tell who was touching me. I'd never even see those two people before. Even after the rescue last time. The guy appeared to be of Asian descent, shorter than Riley, but then again, most were with his gangly six foot probably four by now self. Reaching Riley's shoulder still made the guy tall and if he didn't have the face of a teenager, I'd get confused by the stocky build acquired by adults. The girl by his side had sharp edges to her face, the kind starving models possessed, with hard lines and hazel eyes. Tanned by the sun skin tone and blonde hair pulled back into a set of milkmaid braids.

He sported a crossbow while she had a rifle, one of the kinds used to shoot up schools and kill as many people as it could with less than one pull of the trigger. Why were we going in with little to no protection and no weapons? Was it assumed we were going to use our skills? We had three protection people against all Vince could throw at us?

When I refocused on those in front of me, I saw Imani, eating a granola bar, naturally, as he spoke with Jessa and Peyton. Hands moving, explaining the way rice is properly cooked for all I knew. He'd dug a stocking cap out of his pocket and pulled it snuggly over his shaved head. The cold of nightfall bringing out the crisp air of late fall early winter. I shoved my hands into the pouch of Riley's hoodie and rubbed them together. Here I was ready to storm the castle in my jammies and a set of *All-Stars*, no reason why this wasn't going to end in my demise.

The change of season seemed like a new beginning to me. Even the ones where the leaves changed colors and fell from the trees. The start of school, the first snow of winter, the tulip buds pushing out from the melting snow and the warmth of summer when we no longer had the schedules of school. Each a chance to start new.

This was my chance to start new. Shift with the season. Imani slowed, falling back to where Summer and I were walking.

"Have you checked your backpack?" he asked.

"Let me guess, that's where you found your granola bar and you want mine," I replied.

"If you're offering, sure," he said. "But we're getting close, and you might want to suit up."

"Suit up?" I questioned.

He tapped the bag and I slipped it off my shoulders. Stepping to the side, I stopped by a tree and kneeled. The knee of my pajama pants instantly became damp when it touched the fallen leaves. A bit of dew more than I expected. The sound of the zipper made the others stop and focus on me. In the bag, a perfectly sized outfit matched those of the protection force. Summer and the others followed suit, unpacking outfits that would turn us into a matching set of soldiers.

"What are we doing? Does anyone have a plan?" I questioned, holding up the heavy vest lined with what I could only assume was supposed to protect me from bullets. "Am I supposed to suit up for some battle?"

Why did I feel as if I was the only one being kept out of the loop? Even Imani, having been here less than a minute, basically knew what was going on. Then again, he probably only knew because he'd been searching for food.

"She's right," Riley said. "We do need to change and make sure everyone understands the plan."

For a moment, relief eased the ache in my chest. There was an actual plan, thought out, discussed, planned on a white board somewhere at one time. We weren't going to knock on a door and ask to see Taylor. Were we?

When Peyton and Petra both stripped off their shirts and swapped out for the darker version. I took off Riley's hoodie.

The chill in the air made my skin rise as I pulled the long-sleeved T-shirt over my cami, stuffing the hoodie in the backpack. The weight of the vest bore down on my shoulders in a different way than when it had been in the backpack. No longer pulling me back, it balanced me a bit. The distributed weight helping center me.

Trees were all around us, but not the tall pines of Minnesota I was used to, with branches tapering upward. Instead, I was dwarfed by massive redwoods reminding me how small we truly were in the world. Wandering away from the group to find a bit of privacy, I was able to change my pants without fear of being ogled. The shift from lightweight and flowing pants to heavy duty cargo pants, snug to the body, helped with the feel of control.

Sitting on a fallen tree, I laced up the boots from the bag. Everything fit perfectly. Did they have a set of bags for each of us?

"You okay Aggs?" Summer said as she sat next to me. The dark outfit so out of place for her as her fingers nimbly restrained her hair in a braid. "It was a good thing Sasha was around, huh?"

"Who's Sasha and why is that a good thing?"

Summer pointed toward the sharp angle faced girl who appeared to be recharging as she leaned against a tree with her eyes closed.

"We haven't come up for a name for her skill, but she literally can pull what is needed from thin air. Or maybe she shifts stuff into the right stuff. It's weird. If she hands you a bag, everything you need is right there."

"And yet the keys to a car to get out of here aren't in the bag," I replied, zipping it shut.

"Little One, are you decent?" Imani called from the other side of what had been my modesty tree.

"Depends on your standards, oh Ancient One," I replied.

"Don't make me fight you," Imani said as he approached my log and sat opposite Summer.

"Aren't you supposed to scout ahead?" Summer asked Imani. "Since you decided to randomly join us without being invited."

"You want me to leave?" Imani questioned.

"No," I replied a bit too quick, talking over him as he started to speak on not wanting to cross Vince again. "I'm sorry, continue."

"I was simply saying the last thing I want is to see Vince again. I've been successfully staying in his blind spot for centuries."

"Then why are you helping us?" I asked.

"Because the elders helped me."

"Ms. Weston seems uneasy about being in a group," Summer replied. "As if we were the anomaly."

"Proacting verse reacting." Imani reached into the pouch pocket of his backpack, finding a snack bag size of Cheez-its. "I know you call that *snatcher* a *facilitator*, but honestly that Sasha should be called a *facilitator*."

"Oh, we need to start calling Linc a *snatcher*," Summer said, a grin lighting up her face. "Honestly, that will piss him off so much. Worse than a grabber did."

"He'll stop being the holier than thou praise be to me if we do that." I lightly laughed, thinking of the smug kid we used to pull stuff from catalogs making me wonder if he was a new power. "What did they do back in your day? Did they snatch apples out of a painting?"

"I'd never seen it before, even when photographs began being popular," he admitted. "Then again, those who harness electricity have evolved when currents were discovered. What were random bursts of lighting turned into sustained—"

Imani's eyes closed and lips pursed. The muscle along his jaw ticked, flexing and relaxing. A chill ran through me as if I knew or saw the memory, he'd accidentally triggered by explaining a world that existed before us.

"Summer," Trent called. "Petra might have actually hurt himself."

"It's just a bruise," Petra whined.

"That why you're limping?" Trent prodded.

"I better check him out." Summer stood. "Before Trent gives him an injury he can't avoid."

Her booted feet snapped a few twigs as she walked away. The shake of the bag to my left made me smile as I reached into Imani's bag of salty treats and plucking out a few squares.

"Was your bag full of snacks?" I asked, since he still sported the clothes he came with.

"Mostly, but then again I dress for a fight most days." He reached down and pulled a dagger from the top of his boot. Shifting the weapon from right to left, inspecting the blade before placing it back in its sheath.

"Where did you go?" I asked, then popped the square cracker in my mouth. "Before, when you were talking about electricity."

Imani placed his hand on my knee and patted. "We're not there, Little One. If we are ever there, I may be close to death."

"Vince took me once," I admitted, hoping to build a bridge. "We'd gone to get Taylor to see if she could help with a recon mission and found her. Bruised and frightened, as if Hyde had taken over her sweet Jekyll. I was trying to help Taylor leave. Riley was confronting him, and he knocked Riley out."

"This isn't your first rescue of the child Taylor, then?"

"No," I replied solemnly. "We never officially rescued her last time since Vince took her before we got away."

"And you?" Imani questioned, his tone cold and eyes narrowed. "What did he do to you?"

"Is it worse having it done to you or watching and not

being able to help?" I asked. "I haven't figured it out. Being roughed up a bit, tossed to the side. Smacked. The pain is direct, but—"

A shiver tore through my body and my cheek burned in memory of the hit that sent me flying across Taylor's suite. The crown of my head slammed into the hard steel of the railcar, sending a reverberating ting through my ears. My eyes tried to focus on the petrified Taylor. Already bloodied and bruised with a split lip and swollen eyes when we showed up looking to have her help us. Riley had barely healed her lip when Vince appeared like a twisted nightmare playing out in harsh fashion.

I watched, my stomach turning as he used Taylor's hair to move her around as if she were an untamed horse. Smashing her face to get her to comply as her cries still echoed in my ears. The man she'd stood up for, protected and believed she'd loved. Now beating her within an inch of her life as he and his goons snuck us out of the warehouse in Northern Minnesota. Splashing ice cold water on Taylor to get her to make the car he'd stolen leap. Torturing the skill from her much like mine when petrified.

The car had been sent skidding across a highway in Southern California. Crossing lanes of traffic, thankfully, outside of Palm Springs and between major cities. My scream stuck in my throat for fear of what he would do to me if a sound came from the backseat.

Imani shook me from my thoughts, wiping a tear from my cheek that I hadn't even realized had fallen.

"Both cause scars," he said solemnly and pressed his forehead to mine. "The vision of people in pain haunt our dreams both waking and sleeping while the other comes back with sharp pains of memories."

"What if it's not just Taylor in there? What if—" Another shiver shot through my body and Imani pulled me to him. His arms surrounding me as I crawled on his lap like a small child.

The leather duster he wore swooshed as he wrapped it around like a blanket to cover me. Part of me wished it was a magical cloak whisking me away to a far-off place. Anything to not be here, in this moment, unsure of what I'd be tasked with next. How long had it been since our last battle? A day? It felt like a year. A long, hard year or six even. My power being tested and trained on a crash course with no recovery. Sure, I could have been trying the last month to learn how to yield my shield, but there was so much to do to make our secret world mobile. Worse yet, honestly, I didn't want to accept the power. Never had. Suppressing the idea, I was different or special. While most wanted the powers, to the point of hurting themselves to pull them out. I was the opposite. The last thing I wanted was to stand out.

"Little One, I have seen the strength you possess."

Imani once again broke through my thoughts to bring me back to the here and now. His long fingers running through my hair. I hadn't even noticed I'd lost my binder along the way. If it weren't for the weight of the boots on my feet, I'd think I'd lost my shoes too.

"You said before you knew a shield," I croaked out.

"I did, more than one," he replied, his body stiffening behind me.

"Did?" I question, the vision of Ms. Weston whispering to keep those afraid of their world would never be right again, leading them off the edge of a cliff.

Sitting back, I tried to read his face. The dark eyes soften, as if he could take back the truth of the world. A shield, high, strong, and extension of my own flesh.

"What can pierce my shield?" I asked. "Something must be able to. My hands burned."

"You need your strength," he said, passing me a granola bar.

Staring at the bar, the thought of smacking it out of his

138

hand came to me. Why couldn't anyone give me a straight answer? Imani opened the package and placed the oatmeal and raisin bar at my lips.

"Bite," he said, and I did, but not before cutting my eyes at him. "Little One, who knows if I'm really a *duelist* or I have a commanding tone with good ideas."

Taking the bar from him, I chewed what I'd bit off and swallowed. My stomach instantly growled, demanding more and making his second option of having good ideas have merit.

"The reason your hands burned is because you don't have the hard thick layer you pretend to have," he said. "I've noticed how others react to you. As if you have no sympathy or caring."

"I don't, I'm trying to not die, that's my baseline."

"You're not as ID driven as you like to pretend Agatha dear." The words were matched by his hand sliding along my outer leg, causing a strange scorching heat inside me. "You care for others."

"That's a vicious rumor," I said, though my voice was low and my skin alive. Buzzing in a way as if my shield were in place.

His hand moved, cupping my face to tilt my lips toward him. Our eyes locked and it felt as if I were caught up in a whirlwind. Hot air surrounding me, sticking to my skin, foreboding in a way, as if a tornado was forming hundreds of miles above me in the sky. The dark irises drawing me in and tempting me with what could be. Hiding away, sleeping for decades, until the world came back in balance.

"Hate to break it to you, Little One. You care about people. That is what pierces the skin. It breaks through and coats you because try as you like, you are unable to separate you from the danger. Because you are trying to protect everyone. That is why you push away, fear of letting a person down."

His thumb stroked along my cheek and my stomach clenched. Breath hitching the last thing I was thinking about in the moment was other people. Still holding the granola bar between my thumb and forefinger, the rest of my hand pressed to his chest. Hard and firm, as if he worked out and not with a video game. Imani was a man though, over a thousand years old and it didn't matter if he appeared eighteen, it was wrong to look at him with sick crush eyes, but here I was. Crushing hard for a man, holding me tight, wrapping me up and taking me away from the world into our own little bubble.

Burning and slightly disembodied, I moved closer to him only to realize there was barely an inch between us. The distance vast until my lips pressed to his, only my touch wasn't reciprocated. Cold, stiff lips greeted me, and embarrassment sent me flying. Literally flying backward from my shield, pushing me from him.

"Agatha," he called as the inch turned into twenty feet.

Around me, the hum of my shield mixed with the distortion of my vision. Like an old dirty window, hand blown with bubbles and uneven parts. The kind you saw when you went on tours of historical places. Only on the other side of this window I saw Imani trying to come toward me. Flying at first, then stalking only to be tossed back when he ran into my shield. On the edges, Riley appeared with Gordon. Their words much like Imani's now becoming muffled. It was as if they spoke into a pillow.

Summer came around a tree, her hands splayed. Was she trying to calm me down? Glancing over my shoulder, behind me roots from a giant redwood snapped from the earth as it fell. The edge of my shield forming around what was left of the ancient tree. Fallen because I needed to be away from where I was at the moment.

Who'd seen? Who was wondering what had happened? And more importantly, how could I pull them into my protection as wolves howled in the distance? Their fur a blur as they cut between the trees, their speed greater than any born wild. We must be close because Vince's guards were on patrol and knew we were here, and they were coming for us.

CHAPTER TWELVE

Pointing, I tried to alert my friends, but it was too late. Petra was attacked from behind. Rolling on the forest floor as a wolf clamped onto the back of his neck. Sasha took aim, her rifle releasing bullets with a puff of smoke. The projectile moving slowly across the open space before winging the wolf, who let out a harsh, high-pitched howl before morphing into a woman clutching her shoulder.

Her eyes narrowed, glaring as Summer rushed to Petra to heal the bite marks on his neck. Blood draining along his throat at the same time, congealing under the flesh to form bruises. Before Summer could make contact, his eyes burned, sending laser beams out and silencing the *shifter* by cutting through her flesh as easily as he had the steel rail cars.

Summer slammed on the brakes, her feet kicking upward and sending her falling back on her ass. Her hands were crab crawling backwards to leave space. The instant death one none of us wanted to experience.

Empty eyes stared up from a cauterized head. No longer attached to the body of the woman and more wolves began to circle our group. Dried leaves around the corpse lit up with flames, crackling as they burned. Petra's face lost all color, the young boy turning into a soldier in a split second. His powers had only had a practical use since he'd discovered them. I'd seen him scuffle or fight with other guys, but never murder someone. Never use the power he knew was deadly. The reaction he'd had was completely instinctual, his fight mode activated. Much like my shield currently in place. Survival mode changing a gentle soul into something dark and unsure.

"Petra," I said. "Jacob."

The sweet brown eyes, soft and tender, shy most days and down turned to me.

"Aggs, I—I—it wasn't—"

"Can you control it?" I asked, and he nodded, the blood trickling from his neck as his knee gave out a bit and he placed his hand, knocking off a bit of bark from a tree as he braced himself.

Snarls and snorts turned into yips of pain as a few of the wolves dropped and others tucked tail to run back to Vince's strong hold. We'd been discovered. There was no element of surprise. If anything, we were still at a disadvantage and when Petra dropped fully to his knees, it was Riley who went to his side to heal him initially. Summer only came close when Riley assured her it was safe. Jacob Petra had gone from fun and loving to a threat. It had always been there. Much like Trent could turn venomous or into a creature, deadly enough to get a whole week on an animal channel.

"Aggs," Peyton's voice made it through my shield. "Any chance you could drop the shield or at least let us in? Just in case they come back."

Could I? Either option was strange. Keeping them out or bringing them in. Allowing myself to open the door Claire said was in my heart. Fear had my shield out. No matter where I put my hands I couldn't make it disappear, but how had Imani put it. The shield was like my skin. A layer, one that understood good touch and bad. The bad adult we were told to respect, but our skin crawled when touched. Even their aura would hit you before their hand, warning you of the danger they posed.

Peyton's eyes pleaded with me. This was my purpose, protect my friends. Around me, my shield reverberated. A hum as it engulfed the small glade, partially made from my fear, and completed by space needed for growth. Outside, my friends didn't push or force their want for me to let them in. They waited as time slowed, my mind allowing me to not lower the shield, but extend it. Enveloping each member of our team as if I were hugging them. Pulling them to my lap to comfort them. My skin, the extension of me reaching out to take them into my arms.

"Is he good?" I asked, and Summer nodded, running her hand over Petra's head. "Well, then can someone please explain the damn plan to me?"

"Little One—" Imani said, but I held up my hand to stop him. No one saw; it was between him and me and if he spoke about it now, everyone would know the truth. His eyes though, the gentle soft ones, the ones that comforted me as he held me to him, spoke volumes.

Cheeks burning, I turned away before I allowed myself to feel more than I should. The last thing I wanted to do was retract my shield. Pull it into me and leave my friends behind in the cold. Lowering my hands slowly, I made sure my heart, my center, the axis point of the shield could stay in place and that was what mattered. Wasn't that how Imani explained it? Glancing over my shoulder, his head tilted down in a nod as he stayed toward the edge of my shield. Jessa, Peyton, and the guy from the protection council came over.

"Duke, you brought the tablet, right?" Jessa asked the last person of our party.

"Yeah," he said, setting down his crossbow and removing the tech.

The more words he spoke, the thicker his southern accent was and making me realize I had been keeping to my tight circle.

"See here, we have the cliffside Dr. Evil style castle on a hill." Satellite images appeared on the screen, with a three sixty zoom around. Guess all great and powerful Vince hadn't learned how to avoid modern technology.

"Little more Frank Lloyd Wright style," Jessa said as we took in the home, incorporating nature in its design.

Unlike a castle, this one had floor to ceiling glass walls on the cliffside. Attack from ocean side was already impossible because of the high cliff, but the sunsets had to be stunning. Two levels, with a patio on the roof. The glass reflective so we couldn't see inside. Street view of the home showed the front with a wood panel veneer and rock mixture. The home blending into the scenery and trees around it.

"The bigger thang," Duke said while tapping the screen a few times. "Is this here."

"The garage?" I asked before he swiped, and I saw it was Dr. Evil style.

A blueprint of the home was on file with the county clerk if the moniker in the corner was to be believed. While it appeared the garage was connected to the home, it wasn't a simple pull the car in and park garage. They'd burrowed into the rock bed and created an elevator system. While one could park and step in what appeared to be the kitchen of the home, another option was for the floor to be lowered into a completely sealed area.

"I bet originally they said it would be some sort of wine cellar," Riley said as he approached. "My safe room was completely off book when my mother built it. But with my family, it made sense. This with wall supports and closed off areas—it couldn't be questioned what it was for."

"What if they had it built when we were at war or after the first nuclear bomb was dropped?" Jessa asked. "Preppers, people building fallout shelters, they could have passed it off as that."

"Money takes away questions," Peyton said. "See that seal? This was in the depression era."

At the edge of the scanned blue print the year nineteen thirty-three was embossed. How many disappeared or died in those rooms? Locked away from the sun. A shiver rocked through me, and the shield fluctuated.

"Don't think about it, Little One," Imani said from his place at the edge of my shield. "Whatever it was, block it out."

"Plan," I said holding my breath and hoping to calm myself. "What's the plan?"

"We assume Taylor is underneath," Peyton said. "These are old plans and I doubt any modifications were registered with the county."

"As long as the taxes are paid and they don't want to build a road," Gordon chimed in. "There's very little chance the county even cares who the owner is."

"Any chance you can just lift the corner of the garage and peer in?" I asked and Gordon narrowed his eyes at me, then tilted his head to the side in thought.

"Probably not." Gordon shook his head. "Yeah, I mean unless there's major foundation issues I couldn't without stroking out, probably. And you know, I look like the Hulk, but I only have half his strength."

Flexing his muscle, the rest of us were able to find a little bit of levity. Gordon's strength came from his mind, more than his body. Awkward items like giant plates of steel gave him pause but were as light to him as a clutch purse.

"Honestly, the plan is shot," Peyton said. "There's no need

for stealth. Vince knows about us, so he'll be on guard. We might as well knock on the front door."

"Or some of you knock on the door, and the rest of us use it as a distraction," Imani offered. "Really, if Riley can block the blocker—"

"Last time I saw Vince, he was getting ready to slit me open."

"Yeah, but it's not the right time of the month," Imani said. "It would be a waste to kill you now."

Everyone turned to face Imani, his eyes wide with shock.

"What did I say?" Imani blanched. "I know the stories as well as you do."

"That being said," Peyton continued. "It might actually work."

"Sacrificing Riley?" I questioned.

"No but having our President and VP on a mission of peace at the door," Peyton explained, and Trent's head popped up from its resting place on Summer's shoulder. "While a few of us are working on getting in other ways."

"And how do we explain the people Petra killed?" Trent asked, and I did my best to keep my eyes from taking in the sight just beyond my shield.

"Casualties of war." Riley's distant voice startled me. "Petra was attacked. They should be glad we didn't kill them all. Imani's right, if I keep switching my focus, Vince will have to put all his focus on me, which means the rest of you would be safe. Even Trent could shift, might not be able to shift back when Vince is around, but he could show him how vicious a wolf could be."

Trent had dropped his head in his hands. Shaking from left to right. Summer's hand soothing him with circles on his back. In that moment, I wanted to be back on Imani's lap, his arms holding me and letting me know everything would work out. Instead, fear was trickling down my spine warning me Riley may possibly be taking one for the team. Would we be swapping him for Taylor? Is there anyone I'd be willing to swap for? Was anyone worth that?

"Aggs." Riley's hand touched my shoulder and my shield expanded. The trees groaned in complaint as if hurricane-force winds were bending them. Even with the open space, I couldn't help feeling claustrophobic.

Skin, body, every part of me could feel the rough bark of the tree. Unevenly pressing into my flesh. The smell of fall leaves and old moss stronger than it had been before. Filling my lungs and traveling through my body. Parts of me becoming one with the ground beneath my feet. It hurt, but I couldn't stop myself from sinking deeper. Everyone was backing up further from me.

"Help her," Riley said, laying on the ground and reaching his hand out to me as if that would somehow make a difference.

Was I sinking into the pit of despair? The group was surrounding the edge of the ground, swallowing me.

"Little One," Imani called as he floated above me, then slowly descended to where I was. "Agatha, I'm going to need you to close your eyes."

"No." Shaking my head, I looked around and saw the earth wasn't swallowing me.

While Summer and Trent were above me, I was in a bowl, the forest floor intact with only the loose leaves falling around me.

"We only have about two minutes before the ground gives way and you'll create a sinkhole."

My mind reeled. Trying to envision the gaping holes that appear, swallowing cars, homes and even city blocks. Perfectly carved along the side as if done by a laser beam. Not this bowl with the bottom giving out.

"Right now, you're basically in a colander. The small holes

won't be able to hold and it's going to fall away," Imani continued the confusing description. "Your shield is going to cut a hole, but I've never seen anyone, not even a *shield,* survive the drop."

Imani floated down behind me. His body sliding down my back as his arms wrapped protectively to me. My hands curled around his thick forearms as they crossed my chest, and I gripped the leather of his coat. An anchor finally for my lost self, cocooning me in a hard shell. Smells intermingled with the smaller trees' fallen leaves, leather and sandalwood. Freshly turned dirt seeped in and the vision of the colander had me begin to tremble.

"Shhh," Imani consoled me. "I got you, Little One, even if the ground goes away."

Muffled sounds from the others were distant, and I was afraid to open my eyes. What if the ground was gone? A hole, wide and large, opening up and swallowing the world above. That could have been happening right now. I didn't know. My booted feet were no longer touching the forest floor, bent and warped as it was. Once again, Imani was saving me. First from giving up on myself when I couldn't catch the train. Now from overusing my shield.

"I don't know how to turn it off," I confessed.

"Off, on, all is a mix of fear and love. Those you care for will be shielded, but as long as fear dominates you, it will expand." Imani squeezed tighter around my body, the warmth and security lessening my unease at the unknown. "Riley will be fine."

"You don't know that," I snipped. "Unless you have foresight too, you have no way of knowing that."

149

"I know Peyton wouldn't allow us to come this far if he'd seen a vision."

The trembling threatening to overtake my body slowed. I'd let Peyton into my circle, my shield, my heart in a way one would a brother or friend. Because I trusted him and he wouldn't have come along, not for Taylor, even if it helped eliminate one of our dangers. Furthermore, he wouldn't have suggested the change in the plan. Were there dangers? Yes. Could the future change from his vision? Also yes. But there was a certainty when it came to his visions. Much like a fairytale or folklore. A smattering of truth was in the story, even if it turned on a dime, twisted and ended up a little bit different.

"What do you need, Little One?" Imani asked. "What can I do to ease your fear?"

"Never let go," I said, the words pushing past an acidic lump in my throat. My hands gripped tighter to his arms. His lock around me and mine in his. A double bolted protection around me. The visual reminding me of the seal on the plans.

Opening my eyes to the world the damage I inflicted on clear display. The sedimentary rocks beneath weren't like the ones in cities where construction had blasted through, followed by water over decades eroding the foundation. No, I'd only compressed them, made them stronger. I hope people could think a natural depression happened. Possibly turning into a pond where life could thrive after a good storm. While the basin I'd created was deep, with trees at strange angles I hadn't completely sent the world away below me.

"There's my Little One," Imani comforted as he flew us to the ridge I'd created. "Now can we save your friend?"

"You tell me?" I question as my feet felt ground again, the sturdiness resonating up my legs. A solid foundation settling me into where I needed to be at the moment, even if I wanted to be a million miles away.

"Agatha, I can always fly you away." Imani released his hold on me, and I struggled with letting his arms go for fear of cold. The comfort brought on by a blanket, a good book, and a roaring fire on a snowy night. "We can disappear for decades. I know many ways to blend into a crowd or better yet turn a cave into a home."

Temptation slammed into a wall of guilt and, sadly surety. Surety I wouldn't be able to live with myself if I left behind the people standing around me right now. Riley was the only one who actually knew Taylor. Having grown up with her playing in their backyards. The rest were a group of people believing she was one of ours and therefore, worthy. Much like myself. We were all making mistakes along the way but discovering one's power and self isn't exactly a straight line. Glancing over my shoulder, I took in the very big curve my journey had taken, and still my friends were here for me.

"You think I could smoosh his house and we could dig out those trapped in the basement?" I joked.

Peyton held up a finger, then tilted his head to the side. "You know—"

"No," Riley said. "But we also were only thinking of Taylor. What if there are more?"

"It's not a what if," Imani said, placing his hands on my hips. Probably to keep me from running, but heat seared around my waist and radiated up and down my body. "There will be others."

"Do we have a contingency for that?" Trent asked. "Some might be Satori. We have quite a few unaccounted for between the move and the last take off."

"All that want to come with, come with," Riley said declaratively, and Trent's shoulders stiffened.

"Look, we've wasted twenty minutes. More than enough time for those shifters to make their way back to Vince's home," Peyton said. "Let's discuss the plan B we're pulling out of our butts on the fly."

"I knew you'd never say yes to my offer," Imani whispered in my ear. The light breath tickling and causing gooseflesh to erupt along my skin. "Know this, Little One. The option has always been there for me to leave, but then I met you and your home became mine."

I turned my head, but Imani placed his hand on my temple, forcing my attention back to those coming up with a strategy. One I was a major part of thanks to a vent and the fact only Sasha and I could possibly slip through.

It didn't surprise me Vince lived in a home where the world fell away. While I enjoyed lake homes in Minnesota, unless you were on Lake Superior, you could see across the water to the other side. Not Vince. His home was on a peninsula. Only one way in from land and one misstep would send you to your death. While constructed in the Frank Lloyd Wright style, I couldn't imagine Vince allowing tourists to check out the construction or even registering the home so he must have paid an apprentice. Or blocked the world's knowledge of the real designer. Either way, the tiny vent for fresh air leading to the basement wasn't conveniently along the front face of the home. Nope there was a thin ledge Sasha and I would not only need to walk along but pry off a vent cover once there.

This was our way in, the way out…that was another story that I hoped Sasha's ability to Mary Poppins her bag of tricks would be able to pull off. Peyton explained the best code busting equipment and she nodded in understanding.

We were all passed small earpieces, all but Riley and Trent. What happened with them would have to be told by visual recon. We couldn't take the chance of Vince seeing the communication and if they were going up there, hands out in peace, they couldn't have anything Vince would claim was disingenuous. The man was a *blocker*, not a *reader*. There was a stillness I wasn't expecting from a cliff setting. Shouldn't winds be whipping around from the ocean? Peaceful as the Pacific was supposed to be, didn't mean it wasn't going to have a harsh wind along the surface.

Rubbing my upper arms, I tried to fight off the cold not coming from the air temperature. Unease, I had to hold back my fear, since my shield was nicely tucked away at the moment. Imani turned me as we stood by one of the redwoods at the edge of the official forest. Slipping the hat from his head, he tugged it on mine. Covering my face at first before flipping the skull cap, making it tight to my head as he placed a chaste kiss on my forehead where it was covered.

"My Little One, I will be with you physically until you disappear down that portal."

"It's called a vent," I said, reaching for his hands as our fingers intertwined.

"Yes, but portal sounds more ominous."

"Now you sound like Riley."

"It's a guy thing. Acting as if we were doing something heroic. All the while, the women are handling the heavy lifting. A millennium of living on this planet and I've yet to see you women exert the power you possess."

CHAPTER THIRTEEN

Sounds, like smells, contain memories. Bringing you back to a place and time. Chlorine was one for me, swim lessons. I couldn't have been more than three and yet, the Kidz Bop playing through the radio as we did pizza slices through the water instantly slammed into my ears when I find an overly strong chlorine smell. Certain old phones remind me of the bell at our school. But right now, a sound has sent a bolt of lightning down my back and if it weren't for Imani wrapping me up around the shoulders, I would have completely lost it.

"Shhhh, Little One," he ordered. "We don't need you yet."

Vince's voice, distant as it was carried on the wind as he greeted Trent and Riley. The deep, commanding tone had kept food from those undeserving in his mind in Satori. Now I believe he enjoyed the suffering when he would eat half an apple then toss it to a *Harvey* without enough credits. The gift a near starving kid had to make a choice, humble themselves to the sadist or give themselves a bit of grace and walk away. Either way, Vince won.

I couldn't make out the words, but the tone carried

through the air. Once again, I was clinging to Imani as an anchor.

"Breathe in and out, eyes closed. Once the door is shut we'll move in."

Open or closed, the darkness of the moonless night made it near impossible to see five feet in front of me. I nodded, unwilling to let my voice start what would end up being a barrage of oh hell nos, let me out of here. Fighting that back. Tamping it down, finding my strength. Taylor and I were far from friends, but we both shared a want to keep Riley safe. To protect him and for that reason alone, she deserved this strike. People that sign on to be part of Satori became citizens that had a protective guarantee.

A click from a door closing had my eyes snapping open. Moving to the side of the tree, my eyes followed the black asphalt to the front door as a soft hand took mine and I glance to see Summer has clasped my hand. Why wasn't she coming with? She could easily fit down the vent with Sasha and me.

Why was she being granted a reprieve? The fear in her eyes told the story of why she was out here, and how the last thing she was getting was a pass. We were fighting on two fronts, which meant she was to stay back and take the walking wounded from each direction. Her boyfriend, the young man whose father she saved to earn her freedom, and most importantly, the boy she'd been in love with for over a year. Not her first kiss, but her first in other ways. She spent most nights curled in his arms and now he was behind a door with a sadist.

Then there was me, the person who knew her best, the one who'd had sleepovers and stayed up until we had the uncontrollable sleep deprived giggles. The one she'd told her deepest, darkest secrets to when we were younger. Nothing life shattering or blackmail worthy, but tear inducing still the same. We'd grown apart in many ways since she'd been sent

155

away to the government camps, but the moment she was free, I was who she searched for. The one she wanted to be with to confide in and I had selfishly kept to myself. Citing not wanting to interrupt her boyfriend time, when honestly, I wasn't comfortable with Trent at times. The last thing I wanted was to make her choose between us because I didn't want him and her around me at the same time. And the last thing I wanted was to be blamed for their breakup, worse yet, her hating me when they stayed together.

"What will I do if I lose you both?" Summer's voice scratched and I could see the tears teetering on the edge of her fair lashes. "I almost lost you once and it nearly killed me."

"When?" I asked.

"A few days ago," she said, squeezing my hand tighter.

Had it only been a few days? A handful of hours and in that time Imani had become my anchor. Even now he hadn't released me from his hold, just allowed Summer to have my hand.

"It did?"

"Yes, I was demanding we stop the train, screaming at Trent, trying to find a way to get back there to you."

"You were?"

"It was the worst twenty seconds of my life," Summer said. "Maybe more. Every moment cut through me like razor blades. Look, I get it. I'm loved up with Trent that doesn't mean I don't still need you. We get through this we are taking a standard girls night, okay?"

Holding in the validation, I felt all I could do was nod in agreement. Connections, hope for the future, all of it building strength inside me. Pressure surrounding my heart and telling me my shield was ready to protect those who had done the same for me.

"Keep her safe," Summer ordered Imani, who I could feel nod behind me.

Summer's hand squeezed mine one last time before letting go.

"Ready?" Sasha asked.

Imani released his hold on me and my anchor holding me safe and disappeared. I wobbled a bit at first, my body becoming accustomed to the weight of him on my shoulders and back. Closing my eyes for a moment, I let out a long breath.

"As ready as I can hope to be," I said as she and I made our way to the north side of the home.

Around the side of the garages, careful to avoid the security system Peyton had warned us about. The globes attached to corners he believed would have a few blind spots. Especially along an edge only mountain goats would feel safe trans versing. Short people have tiny feet and right now I was loving my size fives, even in military grade boots. They were small enough to actually give me a whole inch that I didn't want to look down and see.

Imani floated in the air cliff side. Below, I could hear waves crashing into the rocks as the moon brought the tide in. Heart beats thudded in my chest, and I wasn't sure if I put my shield out around Sasha, who was in front of me. If she started to fall, would my shield bring me with her? Not willing to risk it, I followed her, my body pressed flush as my feet were angled sideways in the worst gymnastics beam routine known to man.

Loose pebbles crunched under our boots, lodging into the ridges and making it so our feet couldn't firmly plant down because of the small pellet. Barely two steps in and I had to go back to hard land.

"Little One," Imani inquired.

"I can't with my boots," I stated, and started fumbling with the laces. "It's too narrow and I need at least my toes to try and grip."

Sasha turned just her head back to look at me. Already a

good four feet on the ledge, the decision one she wasn't ready to back track. She would go forward while I stuffed my boots into my backpack and made sure it was balanced evenly on my shoulders.

With a deep breath, I stepped forward, stocking feet not slick and allowing my toes to curl when needed. In keeping with the home matching the world around it, the garage wall wasn't a smooth surface. No, it had varying degrees of nature carved stones. Sedimentary rocks with layers unevenly spaced having been worn down by wind and rain. If one wanted to, they could boulder this with a good pair of mountain climbing shoes and strong fingers. I had neither and knew if I glanced down, I'd be frozen. Instead, I could only focus on what was at eye level. Pain randomly shot up my leg if I moved it with too much force, catching a jutting stone to the shin. Even if it wasn't quick, the scraping along my calf dug into the bit of flesh I had. No warmth dripped down my leg and while I had pressure, there wasn't the sting from a slice. All the indications that I hadn't cut myself, though the idea Vince would randomly insert razor blades, did cross my mind.

While the pebbles pressed into my feet, at least I could try to brush them away. Sharp jabs had me push up on the ball of my feet, hoping to minimize the damage. How long had it been since I had summer feet, the kind you could run across hot pavement, through grass and even on gravelly trails without even so much as an ouch. I'd only accomplished them the one summer when my mother ran away to a cabin up north. The year after my father was gone, and she needed to regroup. Now my feet were sensitive, and I needed to find a way to speed up my progress.

Sucking in my belly, I held my breath, curving my back slightly in hopes of not having an even worse jolt to my abdomen. The last thing I needed was a slice of a sharp edge giving me an impromptu appendectomy.

Riley and Trent could only distract Vince for so long. The Dr. Evil in him pontificating his greatness at some point would end, and my fear of falling to my death had to be pushed aside. I could tremble and quake as long as I kept moving.

"You got this, Little One," Imani said behind me and I wanted to have him put his hand on my back.

A tether, but then again that might give me too much confidence and I'd make a mistake. My foot falling away beneath me and alerting whatever and whoever Vince had around the place for security. The tightrope I was walking wasn't metaphorical at the moment, and fear had its place in life. Like when you met that bad person your parents tried to tell you was safe. Imani was right—follow that fear, that unease, the twisted gut to the natural conclusion.

"I see the vent," Sasha said, her hands splayed on the wall. "Well, feel it more, my foot found at least an inch indent."

"Gee, and we thought this would be hard," I replied.

"Any chance your boyfriend would be willing to prop you or me from behind because we're gonna have to squat to this and I'm not sure I have the balance for it."

"Um, he's—"

"There is a reason for me," Imani said, but I couldn't see his face.

My eyes were fixed on the layers of rock, thinly sliced and compressed. How many had formed over Imani's lifetime? How many would form over mine if I survive? In that moment, the fear hit like a cold wave crashing into me from the North Shore of Lake Superior. Not because Imani's hands were on the small of my back or my knees were bending as I lowered myself. Unlike the yolo lifestyle of only living once, I had a thousand lifetimes ahead of me. Imani and I could disappear into the vastness of the world, and here I was about to dangle my ass off a cliff with the potential of ending it before I hit two decades.

Sasha slipped a Phillip's head screwdriver the exact size of the screws holding the vent in place.

"No mini drill?" I asked, balancing myself and not trying to depend on Imani floating behind me. His hands were trembling, and I wonder if flying and floating were two very different things. Everything he'd done with me had been motion, moving through the air, then gliding in for a landing. Was it like treading air instead of water?

Shaking my head, I focused on the task at hand as Sasha shone a flashlight on the screws. Slightly rusted, years of salted sea air fusing them with a crusted white dust. They cried out in a harsh metallic tone at first, frightening me with a noise probably not near as loud as I thought it was. The last thing I needed was the echo off the cliff below to send the sound forward. Imani's hands slipping when I jumped didn't help either.

My biggest challenge was keeping my heart slowed and my mind off the dangers all around me. Thinking about the fall, the sea crashing and the chance one of the shifters would turn into a pterodactyl and swoop over to pluck me from this very narrow ledge. Nope, I had to tell myself I was trying to sneak in my house's basement window. There wasn't thirty feet and jagged rocks below me. I should be sitting on the soft grass instead of squatting. Who knew if my thought replacement would actually work? It was until the first screw was out and it tumbled, bouncing off the small ledge and disappearing into the empty void behind me.

Breathing became rushed. Slamming my eyes shut, I knew there was no way to hear the drop when it bounced off the rocks below. Not over the sound of smashing waves, or maybe that was the blood rushing in my ears. Isn't that what my teacher told me when I held a conch shell to my ear? It wasn't the ocean I was hearing.

"You need another screwdriver?" Sasha asked, and I shook

my head. The handle of the other she gave me was imprinting in my palm because I'd pressed so hard to get the screw to loosen and now I was gripping the handle with pinched fingers.

Getting the second off required me to press my left hand on the vent for balance and to get the metal grate even. The screw tight, but once I was able to get it moving, it fell away as the first had. A crash sounded in the house and Sasha slipped from her spot as if pushed. The flashlight tumbling away as Imani's hands left from behind me and I tried to grip the rock wall only to understand what sent her flying backward.

Me. The shield popping out and while I included Imani in my protection, Sasha had been pushed to the side. The best I could do was press my hands flat on the cut out for the vent and balance. Arms burning, abs on fire and the squat I was in had my knees feeling as if they were in need of replacement after two decades in the NFL. The boots I'd removed now weighing my back down.

"Imani, I'm not sure I can hold on much longer," I cried out, unsure if he could actually hear me since I was facing the wall.

"Pull the damn cover," he hollered, and I summoned courage.

Painted over and stuck from decades of not being moved, I had to pound on two of the corners before my nails could get enough of an opening my fingers could follow. Sharp pinching had me pulling with all my might. The balancing act of the ages as the grate loosened and fell on my knee. Heavy, made of a steel I assume before it bounced on my left foot smashing the last three toes and the top of my foot.

Screaming out in pain expanded my shield and Sasha's hand shot out from behind me to cover my mouth. Imani now held her and me up and I could only allow tears to fall. I nodded my head and tossed the damn grate, hoping it shattered into a million pieces as it fell.

In front of me, a square black hole gave me an out into an abyss. There was no other way to go from my position than forward. Arms forward as if I were diving, my knees cracked as I pushed up and forward, only to have my feet break away bits of the wall and float up in the air. I slid down the tight metal portal, choosing Imani's word because it was ominous.

Thank goodness for my backpack, or I would have been uncontrollable. Instead, the backpack helped slow me down enough I wasn't careening out of control and when my hands were pressed to flat concrete, I actually had to move them back to push against the wall to get out. Rolling in the darkness, I flipped the backpack off and dug in the bag, sure I'd find a matching flashlight to the one that had fallen away moments ago. Small, but with a bright LED light, I shone it around a small room and covering my own mouth with my hand to hold back the scream when the light hit the hole I'd come out of. Bright white reflecting in Sasha's eyes making them near translucent and having her waving at me to stop blinding her.

How had I not expected her to be making her way out of the same place I had just come out of? Imani was gone now. Sasha and I were on our own to explore, fight, and rescue. I returned to the backpack to pull out my boots. The right foot slid on with no resistance. The left was already swollen causing me to have to loosen the laces, and once I put weight on the ball of my foot, I saw stars from the pain searing up my leg.

Now free from the portal, Sasha stood and pulled a second flashlight from her bag. Swooping around what would be a vestibule in most places. There were only two doors, one with the electronic keypad Peyton had expected and one simply looking at caused my body to tremble. It was less a door than an iron gate leading to a long hallway.

Dropping to a crouch, I made sure to put most of my

weight on my right foot and pressed my hand to the wall. My foot was broken, of that I had no doubt.

"Your shield still working? Or was that a toss the third wheel off the edge?" I couldn't tell if Sasha was joking or serious. The girl had a poker face.

"Must have been a void in Vince's block," I surmised because fear and unease shot through my body, but the uncontrollable power refused to appear.

"Do you need me?" Sasha asked.

"Where would you go?" I questioned, the cold fear leaching over my body.

"Peyton's lock picker is great, but not fast," Sasha said, pulling the code breaking electronic from her bag. "Once this is open, I can follow. He has no guards down here, so this is simple rescue and run."

"In a nightmarish hellscape." My head feverously nodded as if I was psyching myself up to go inside. My safety anchor was outside, then again, he would end up being triggered seeing what I knew had to be down the hall. Cells, similar to what he had once been tortured inside.

"Your foot?" Sasha asked as I pushed myself up and bent my left foot to balance on the toe of my boot.

"Yeah, won't really be a run, more of an uncoordinated hop."

"Doubt you'll be the only one with a limp." Sasha nodded her head toward the gate.

Centuries had not changed Vince if the smell leaching from the hallway was any indication. The putrid smell of bodily fluids hadn't made its way up the vent. No, it hung in the air, humid and thick. By the time I opened the gate, I had to cover my nose and mouth. How was I supposed to find anyone when even my eyes were burning?

Everything in me told me not to shine the light on the walls, the beam zig-zagging directly in front of me until I saw the end of the hall. Stomach turning as the taste of rotten flesh coated the inside of my nose, causing me to gag as it hit the back of my throat. Bile and acid burning their way up my chest and into my mouth, I swung around to head back to the opening when the beam cut across the doors.

Windows were cut out, like old prisons, maybe six inches by six inches. Inside the square were metal bars so even if one wanted to, their hands couldn't reach out. What had my stomach tightening, vicelike to the point I feared I'd be doubling over, was no one was peering out. Were they restrained or cowering in a corner, praying they wouldn't be the one chosen?

"Taylor," I said, though I'm not sure her name actually made it out of my mouth. "Taylor, please be down here."

"Who's there?" a voice whispered behind me, and I spun on my heel.

The light causing the face in the window to recoil, and I pointed it down. Enough to glow, but not enough to blind the poor person. They reappeared, one eye swollen completely shut, the other staring at me, nearly disembodied from the being attached.

"Aggie?" the person questioned, and I stepped closer.

"Taylor?" I replied.

"No, she's across the way, the last door," they said. "The biggest room, but not because she's being honored."

Glancing over my shoulder, I saw a sliver of light glowing from inside.

"It's Alex," he said. "Downstairs neighbor in the serial killers."

I'd been so caught up trying to help where I could with the transition to the mobile Satori, I hadn't even noticed Alex hadn't been around. Everyone was helping. I assumed he'd been assigned a task. We barely spoke and a part of me felt guilty for not even noticing the absence. Or had he been captured in the train attack? Was this what it was like when older people came back together for reunions? People you hadn't even noticed were gone, even though you used to pass them in the halls every day?

"All these doors? Do they each have a different person locked away?" I asked, doing a quick count, nine on each side.

"Persons," Alex corrected. "My roommate—he's still breathing, but he hasn't moved in over a day."

"If they can't move, we can't help them," I stated even though it left a sour taste in my mouth as I lifted the heavy bar locking Alex inside. "We don't have the resources."

Now I could hear the shuffling of people coming to the window, their cries as they realized they were being saved. Pulling on the door, it had to weigh at least thirty pounds and Alex couldn't help me. Beyond the swollen eye, his shirt was tied into a makeshift sling holding one arm pinned to his body. Still, he moved to where the person trapped with him lay on the floor of the prison cell with little more than a hole cut into the floor in the corner. Circular, but smaller than what was cut into a lake when people ice fished. Max, that thing was six inches in diameter and if boys missed the bowl with a real toilet, this hole in the ground was surrounded by what didn't hit the mark.

Bringing my hand to my face, I held back the gag from the foul odor. The room, windowless, with not even an old wool blanket on the floor for mattress, was poured concrete. Bowls were on the floor, empty, with remnants of an oatmeal or gruel coated to the edges. If I held my arms out, my fingers could touch each side of the room. Over the years, I'd researched inhumane treatment in some attempt to quell my worry for my father. At least he got time out of the cell. They didn't hose him down and beat him regularly.

"He's not waking," Alex said, placing his good hand on my

shoulder to turn me back to the hallway. "Let's go, there are others we can save."

"Aggie? Is that Aggie? Alex, let me out, come on man you know I didn't mean it." Voices mixed and mingled, bouncing off walls because there was no place to go.

My foot numb at this point, I limped, lifting the locking bars as Alex tugged with his good arm. Others followed suit, helping those that could walk, as I made my way to the furthest corner room, the luxury suit Taylor stayed in. I pulled the door open I saw her. Shadows cast around her with one dim light from a candle. The wax pooled beneath it, the wick nearly gone, the flame struggled to keep lit and not be fully engulfed by the melted liquid.

Taylor's skin was translucent. If not for the bruising pattern made by a hand to her upper arm, I wouldn't even be able to make out any definition. Bare, with only a pair of panties on, she was curled into a ball with her arms wrapped tightly around her knees.

This room was larger, but it was because it held Vince's toys. Torture devices were hung on the wall, blades, whips, pointy things and stuff you paid extra to see at Medieval Times. A pear-shaped object, finger locks and chastity belts were sadly the tamer items. Her room was larger because there was a rack in it, which meant he could bring others in here for her to watch as he tortures them. Glancing at Taylor's ankle, a metal shackle had her trapped to the wall. Her eyes were fixed on the flame, not even acknowledging I was in the room. Slipping off my backpack, I retrieved Riley's hoodie and kneeled beside her.

"Taylor," I said, trying to keep my voice soothing because I worried she would jump right out of her skin if my voice was harsh.

"He comes when it's gone," she said, voice unconnected to

her body as the words escaped her mouth. "He comes when it's gone."

"Who? Who comes?" I asked, placing my hand on her hair, thin, lifeless and falling out with the slightest touch. Though cut too short to truly snarl, stress had it falling from the root. "Taylor, is there a key in the room for your shackle?"

Her eyes stay fixed forward and I wish I had someone with super strength or a laser to cut the dang thing from her ankle. Only we were in Vince's home, his power to block greater than any we could conjure up. Even now, I tried to remember Alex's power, only I know it would be useless to him.

Lifting Taylor's arms, I pulled Riley's hoodie over her head, and she instantly returned her arms to her legs. The metal on her ankle had bruised her foot and calf, but when I moved it, the latch fell open. He had her trapped in her own mind. Nothing more, nothing less. She'd been conditioned to sit in this spot. Not to wander further than her own little potty hole and stare at a candle. One that popped slightly, then the light diminished, and we were thrown into darkness.

My skin rose as I prayed my eyes would become accustomed to the pitch black. Only Taylor stole hope from me. Her voice broken as deep as her spirit, cutting through the darkness with a stab as sharp as a knife.

"And now he comes."

CHAPTER FOURTEEN

Light is gone, Taylor is disassociating from whatever Vince has in store for her and at that moment she was a rag-doll and not because she'd lost twenty pounds she didn't have to lose. Pulling her up and dragging her from the room wasn't hard. There was no fighting with Vince, and that meant whoever placed their hand on her could control her like a *Barbie* doll. I might as well be bouncing her around by the waist to take the elevator in the dream house.

The hallway was empty, but I could hear the voices in the vestibule. Waiting, demanding, acting as if we hadn't just rescued them when I was only sent to get Taylor. The ungrateful orders being yelled at Sasha as she stood, cable connected to the electronic lock as numbers and sequences emitted a greenish blue light in the room.

"Taylor knows, have her punch it in," one girl called out, her left eye drooping and cheek purpled to the point it was black on her tanned skin. Lip busted and cuts along her exposed upper arm like hash marks showed she was beaten, but not broken. Fight bubbled in her in a way I envied until I thought of what had that rage bubbling.

Taylor's eyes were vacant, and I thought of Ms. Weston, leading those off the cliff because they could never be well again. Not mentally, and while we have therapeutic theories, no one in Satori is trained for it. We are trying to get through our own issues. Helping others work through what was done to them wasn't exactly something we were equipped for. Taylor hadn't even acknowledged me, the hoodie she was wearing or where she was in the world.

Taking her face in my hands, I turned her toward me. One time enemies, then associates at best. We fought over Riley a bit, her to protect her friend and me, unsure what I wanted beyond food and another human in the room with me while watching TV.

"Taylor," I said. "Do you like Riley's hoodie?"

Her eyes blinked and head turned slightly.

"You know you're wearing it? Can you smell the soap he likes?"

Light was returning to her eyes. Would I be bringing her back too quickly? Would she collapse?

"There it is," I said, letting go with one hand to bring the fabric at the neck up to her nose. "Didn't he steal your ball and be your best friend?"

"No, no." Taylor's head began to shake. "No, he can't. Vince has traps."

"What did the zombie girl just say?" Sasha asked.

"That Vince has traps," I replied. Our eyes locking because currently we were stuck with only one way out. How had I not thought of this as a suicide mission?

"Yeah, and this keypad has a seven digit code," Sasha said. "Seven, which means we could be here for days."

"He comes when it's out," Taylor's voice said, deep in warning.

"When what is out?" Sasha asked.

"A candle," the random girl with the busted face said. "He

comes when it goes out. We can always tell when it happens because Taylor's shackles scrape."

"It's out?" I said. "But Riley and Trent—"

"Might be in one of his traps," Sasha said, cutting me off and snatching the fabric surrounding Taylor and manhandling her to the keypad. "Do you know the code?"

The strong Taylor I'd met six months ago had been decimated. Quick witted, smart, willing to take me out if Riley sharing an apple would mean he was hungry. Buried inside her, covered in the scars, we couldn't see she had to exist. Didn't she? You couldn't completely take away who a person was deep down, could you?

Removing Sasha's grip on Taylor's hoodie, I placed my hands on her upper arms or what was left of them. I thought Claire was waif like, but Taylor's upper arms were basically bone covered in skin making my own flesh crawl the moment I found them beneath the thick sweatshirt material. Tears came to my eyes, wishing I could take away her pain. Our past fights disappeared when I looked at the human being before me. My heart shattered, and I had to push past the thousands of images bombarding my mind of what she might have gone through. The instruments of torture that lined the walls, reminding her in candle cast shadows of all the ways she may find pain once the light was extinguished.

Her fingers were playing with the string from the hood of the sweatshirt. Broken nails with chipped polish rolling the knotted end between the middle finger and thumb. A soothing ritual starting, the muscles in her face relaxing as she brought the twine to her nose.

"Riley and I have the same birthday?" she mused whimsically. "Do we all have the same one? Us special ones?"

"No," I replied, not knowing Riley or her birthday, but knowing Summer and I were three months apart. "I was born in May."

I rubbed my hands up and down on Taylor's upper arms, then walked her to a corner and helped her sit down. Only she didn't sit. She squatted and leaned her head to the side on the wall.

"She's lost it," another guy said. "We all know it. She'll sing songs in her cell. Like kid songs."

"We've got one number, one," Sasha said. "We've been here fifteen minutes? This thing is calculating millions of possibilities per second and still one number. Each one is going to take a minimum of fifteen minutes and could take double."

"Seven numbers, even at fifteen a piece, we're looking at two hours minimum," Alex said.

"We don't have that kind of time." I shook my head. "Is there any other way out?"

"How did you get in?" Alex asked.

"Vent." I thumbed behind me to the small opening.

"We could crawl back up it, couldn't we?" another girl asked, sticking her head inside.

"First, it's steep, like almost a straight garbage chute drop," Sasha said. "Crawling up, even with someone pushing you it would be next to impossible."

"Then there's the cliff wall," I added.

"Cliff wall?" Alex asked.

"We're on a cliff, big rocks on the bottom, followed by crashing waves from the ocean. We're at least fifty feet up."

"So we're careful when we get out, belly crawl." The girl inspecting the size of the opening added.

"The ledge is less than four inches," I said. "I only know that because I did gymnastics for a year and I can tell you, the beam was wider."

"Vince loves numbers," Taylor said, her voice sing song as she began humming the birthday song.

"I swear on all that is holy if I never get wished a happy

birthday it will be too soon." Alex ran his good hand through his hair.

"Summer and I call ourselves ying-yang twins," I mused.

"That's great," Alex snipped, then went do the panel. "Where does this even open up?"

The wall was smooth, only a thin line in the shape of a door. Did it fall away, slide into the wall or get sucked up into the celling?

"You don't remember?" Sasha asked.

"We're brought down with hoods over our head," a boy said as he rested, leaning in a corner. "I woke up in my cell, so they must have carried me down."

"What kind of powers do we have here?" I asked.

"None," Alex said, rage burning from him to the point the room's temperature seemed to rise. "None of consequence anyway. Do you see me short circuiting the panel? Nope, just like I couldn't electrocute Vince when he twisted my arm until my shoulder popped out."

"Summer?" a girl with fire red hair asked, her arm obviously deformed from a bad break who I could tell wasn't putting any weight on her right leg at all. "The healer?"

"Yes, we're best friends from before," I said.

"Fine, I'll bite. How are you ying-yang twins?" the boy in the corner asked. "Blonde hair, brown hair?"

"No, I was born on May second," I said, and Taylor's voice got louder on the birthday song. Playing on loop as if someone hit repeat instead of shuffle on their iPod. Glancing at her, I shook my head and continued. "She was born on February fifth. Two five, five two. Same year, ying-yang."

"*Happy birthday to you. Happy birthday to you. Happy birthday day, dear blessed ones,*" Taylor sang, her voice bouncing off the walls. "Two five, five two, seven three, three seven, six nine, nine six. No late month babies."

"What did she just say?" Sasha asked, as Taylor began another rousing round of happy birthday.

"No late month babies?" I repeated, my eyebrows knitting together in confusion.

"Was anyone here born between the thirteen and the end of the month?" Sasha asked, and everyone shook their head. "So in theory we'd all have a ying-yang twin that was an *aberration?*"

"Seven three, three seven," Taylor repeated, the song gone from her voice. "Three seven, seven three, seven three, three seven."

Her endless birthday loop had turned into a loop of reflective numbers. Over and over.

"You don't think?" I said, not willing to voice my guess out loud, as if any option would be wrong.

"If I stop the sequencing, we'll have to start from the beginning."

"And still," I said, then went to Taylor and sat cross legged by her. "Taylor, when is your birthday?"

"Seven three, three seven."

"You and Riley were almost independence babies. The Yankee Doodle kind born on the Fourth of July?"

"Seven three," she said, smiling a bit and bringing the twine to her lips for a light kiss. "Different twins, not to be forever mated. Vince tells me secrets, secrets even Peyton doesn't know."

"Like what?" I ask hoping to find the code buried in the insanity that was Taylor's ramblings.

"Seven three, three seven. Three, seven, seven three. He can't help himself. Best bonds blend, meld into one." Her fingers dropped the string and interlocked together. "Did you know, seven three seven. Three seven three."

Taylor once again got lost in the numbers repeating on a three number loop now.

"Did she drop the repeating number?" Sasha asked.

"Yeah, she did," I replied. "What if—" I had to give my theory now. There were no other options. "We need seven numbers. It could be their birthdays, melded."

"Which way? She keeps changing?"

"How many incorrect codes until it locks us out or sounds the alarm?" I asked, adrenaline surging through my body, making me anxious as I bounced a bit on my right foot.

"I won't know until I enter a code," Sasha replied. "I probably will say you have three more times until you're locked out or something."

"Do we keep it two thousand at the end? Or one thousand? Because seven three seven or three seven three only gives us four more numbers."

Sasha snatched the connecting cable from the lock and my heart clenched tight. No breath entered my lungs as her fingers went for the first sequence. Seven, three, seven, two, zero, zero, zero. The harsh alarm beeped, and we all took a collective step back.

"We get three shots," Sasha said, her fingers trembling as she pressed the three on the screen.

"Which means one more," I commanded, and she glanced over her shoulder. "One more, then go back to Peyton's thingamajig."

"At this point, let them come," Sasha said, turning back and hitting the seven button again.

"What if they don't come?" I replied. "What if the floor rises up or the walls squish together? They couldn't find real plans for this place. It could be a death trap."

"Then let us die." The roommate of Alex fell from the hallway when he stopped leaning on the wall.

Rushing I caught him before he fell, sending pain shooting up my left leg that had been numb, reminding me it was still broken. The smell of rot and decay filled my nose with a fresh bouquet of disgust. His skull caved in on the left side like the forest where I'd indented the ground. They want to die, fine. Who was I to judge, but I wasn't ready to end it all. Life was beyond that door, and for the first time, my anchor was out there. Beyond the door, perched, waiting to swoop in, literally, to help us. Rescue us. Rescue me.

Taylor stayed in her squat position but waddled toward me. "He can't help himself."

Was this some domestic abuse survivor crap going on? Making excuses for why she was being beaten.

"Like the cave, remember the cave, he was drawn to it, we all are."

Balancing between caring for the half dead guy in front of me and letting Taylor run off at the mouth with insanity wasn't my favorite way to spend an evening. Sadly, it was where we currently were.

An alarm pierced my ears, but Taylor didn't even move, she only held her tongue until it stopped.

"Every month, it calls to us," she continued. "And we are called to our other half. He's called to me. I can't get away. He'll always come for me."

"What about others born on March seventh?" I asked. "Are they called to you too?"

Her eyes widened and for a moment, I thought she might have seen hope. Processing my words, she began smacking at the side of her head with her palm. The repeated pattern of seven three, three seven running at nauseum from her as Alex dropped to a knee by me to take over care of his roommate. Allowing me to switch back to Taylor babysitting, as I caught her by her wrists.

"Three, seven, three, zero, zero, number two." The words flew in rapid succession.

"That's only six," Sasha said, staring at the screen.

"Second place." Taylor closed her eyes and shook her head.

"Don't old people say hashtags are number symbols?" I asked, and Sasha stared at me. "Like on a phone. My mom was confused when I said hashtag at first."

"I thought it was a pound," Sasha said, but hit the back button on the screen twice.

"Pencils, they're hashtag two," Alex added. "But we call them number twos."

Excitement began building in the room. All of us trapped, with broken words from a shattered mind, laying out a puzzle with a thousand pieces. The corners found, the edges complete, but now we needed that one piece that fell under the table.

"Last chance," Sasha said, as she pressed the hashtag button at the bottom of the keypad, followed by the two.

CHAPTER FIFTEEN

Lights flickered above us. My own eyes had become accustomed to the darkness. For those that had been imprisoned molelike there was a collective cry as they brought forearms to cover their eyes. Taylor hissed and turned her eyes down to the floor to avoid the florescence above us.

Sasha was the only one focused directly ahead. The outline of the door expanding as it disappeared down into the floor.

"Everyone out, I don't know if this thing has a timer," Sasha commanded, but stood sideways in the doorway with her foot planted firmly to where the door had disappeared into.

Shuffling past her, the imprisoned helped each other if the need was there. Hope, caring, just like Riley preached to his mother. Abandoning each other would be simple. Can't keep up, that's on you, but that wasn't who we were. Glancing down the dark hallway, I wondered who was left behind. I knew about Alex's roommate but refused to look in the other rooms for those who may have been left behind.

"*Happy birthday to you,*" Taylor began singing again, shaking me from my thoughts.

"You coming Aggs?" Sasha asked, and I pulled the songstress Taylor from her crouched position.

The chorus laden song keeping us in step until she got to the door and stood stick still.

"Taylor, we need to go," I said, trying not to tug too hard on her hand.

"I can't do it again," she said, shaking her head. Tears would be streaming, but I was afraid she was dehydrated. "You can't—I don't want to."

"Taylor," I took both of her hands in mine trying to lead her over the threshold. "We're going to see Riley."

Her hands slipped from mine, and I had to cross back over to capture them again.

"The floor is vibrating," Sasha said and made sure she was outside of the vestibule following the others.

"Help me," I said, trying to grab Taylor, only to have her hands smack me away. If she ran, I couldn't chase her, my foot was too damaged.

Lunging forward, I tackled her and glanced over my shoulder to see the door was returning, moving up slowly to get back in place. Tackling Taylor, I spun her around. Stabbing pain jutting up my leg, but now wasn't the time. I was going to dog walk her if I had to, but strength from the adrenaline, fear and pisstivity had me stepping through the opening. My foot catching on the raising door and sending me flying forward with Taylor as my surfboard.

Bracing myself for the impact, time slowing to the point I wondered if the pain of impact would be greater. When my hands hit the floor would the locked at the wrist pose I was in shatter them or would they crush up into Taylor's belly and have her vomiting? The air became static and the distance between my face and concrete unmoving as I opened my eyes to see my shield in full force, wrapped around Taylor and me, a cushion of air resting on the floor.

Rolling to the side, we were lowered to the floor and my shield disappeared.

"How?" Alex asked, flicking his good fingers as if his power just needed a good restart.

"I don't know," I said honestly. "Vince has said in the past he forgets about me. Maybe that's how. I know outside it didn't work."

Crammed into a smaller space, people were sitting on the stairs to make room. Only they couldn't go more than five stairs from the top because it led directly into a ceiling. This was basically a root cellar, and we needed to flip the doors. A few were pressing with all their might, and it didn't even budge. At some point air, heat and musk from the unwashed was going to overpower us all. Even now, I wasn't sure if chemical warfare wasn't being used, since we all were sipping air to avoid breathing in the funk.

"What was the next part of the plan?" I asked Sasha right before a loud boom caused the ceiling to tremble.

"That," she replied as car alarms echoed above us as harsh as the alarm from before, but without the ability to stop the noise as it pierced our ears.

Scraping on the ceiling had those on the stairs rushing backdown and making a small space tighter. If my shield could appear from me falling, it had to appear now. Only then I'd been saving Taylor, making sure she got through when her lost mind feared whatever Vince would make her do. Unable to stay on the same plane of existence as the rest of us for more than a few moments. She hadn't been trapped with Vince long enough to be this trained, had she? One month, maybe a bit more, sure there was the grooming period when she'd fallen for him. Puppy love at best. What did I know? I hadn't known love. Friendship, a little bit of attraction at best. And by the birthday standard, would that mean Summer was my soulmate? All of it to confusing and too many thoughts hitting me at once.

Pushing my way past everyone, I needed air, I needed space and the only place where that existed was on a set of wooden stairs leading to nowhere. The scraping, explosions and now a bit of yelling above me aside, I could sit on the step, fourth from the top and be perfectly content. Arguments happened at my home, and I'd sat idle on the steps. My mother tossing breakable things at my father, who would move enough to let them smash. In the morning, I'd go in search of new dings and dents in the wall. They were always where you didn't expect them.

Pressing my palm flat to the wall, I allowed myself to get lost in the feel. Closing my eyes like I did when I was a kid by an elevator. Wondering if I could figure out the braille, but never applying myself enough to even do word association like one would when learning a new language. The poured concrete wall was cold, smooth, the only imperfections ones made by the trowel or mold. There wasn't the jagged edges like there had been outside where they were keeping it with the natural look. An extension of the cliff to confuse and camouflage. Or perhaps it was to not steal the beauty of nature with human's influence.

No matter the reason, it was false. The inside is what matters, the heart of the home. This one was cold, vile, and dark. Much like its owner. The coolness only soothing from the point we were trapped by heat. The panel above me couldn't be much, but we were below a garage and the chance a car was above me was great.

Resting my cheek on the concrete, I tried to block out the world. Upset below and above. Odor and, most importantly, the muffled voices that gave me a headache. I wanted to think about Imani and Riley, both helping me in their own ways. Riley giving me strength and Imani showing me how to pull my power from deep inside me. Not rushing or tossing me into the danger hoping to illicit a reaction. Rubbing my middle finger and thumb together, I went back to the beginning. Playing with a shield in private, not even knowing what it was at the time. Much like my Barbies, I'd put my childish games away, but those games were meant to teach me how to be as an adult.

Imani let me find my strength, buried deep inside as I pulled those I cared for in, even Taylor. Glancing down the stairs, I realized my bubble was back, and that's why I hadn't been able to see it in just my palm. The distortion beyond the edges evident, but it was the muffled voices. The shifting of my foot on the wooden stair echoed and reverberated inside my safe space. None of the others could use their powers so how could I? Imani had said I was more powerful than even I knew, but more powerful than Vince? No. A hard thump above me made the panel bounce, but more importantly my shield expanded.

The ground, the spot in the forest, had the local sedimentary rocks underneath it had to. Even if it didn't, at some point dirt has to turn into rock. Which means I had the power to not only bring those behind me in, but blast whatever car was sitting on the panel away.

Turning I knelt on the third step, my hands flat a few inches from the panel above me as I pushed. Not with my arms but expanding my shield. My heart blowing up as if I were the Grinch and Cindy Lou Who invited me to dinner. Behind me were friends, and Alex called out to me unafraid. There was no thought that I was part of Vince's sick lacky crew because he knew me. Briefly meeting me and yet it was enough for trust to be built. A trust I'd been told to ignore as false when honestly my perception of people had been spot on for most of my life even if I denied the positives at first.

Closing my eyes, I envisioned Summer and me at the lake.

Pretending we were so grown as we wore oversized hats and dangled our feet off the pier. Her telling me secrets in the hallway, as she braided my hair, and we watched the older kids playing soccer.

Then Riley, the heat of his body as he sat next to me on the couch as we were being shuttled to the camp. Again, I fought my instincts when it came to him, the positive vibes, until he literally wouldn't allow me to push him away anymore. Forcing me to accept a friendship and I let myself go, kissing him like a fool when I saw he was still alive.

And then Imani, the third leg in my safety stool. Staying because of me, to protect me when the first thing I did was question if he should be tossed off the train. The thought not in my heart, but a knee jerk reaction to my attraction to him. I didn't want any doubt. I didn't like being drawn to him and wanting his warmth. Now I yearn to have my anchor holding me steady and telling me I was safe because he was there. He would protect me, even when I was the dangerous one.

Above me more than a panel burst forth and splintered, and half the ceiling fell away. Debris covering the top of my shield was a mix of wood and concrete. Those behind me safe in a bubble, they hadn't even noticed as it expanded and protected them. Weren't those secret protections the best?

"How can she fight Vince's blocking?" someone asked behind me.

"Who cares," Sasha replied. "Stay behind her and let's go."

The SUV that had been resting on top of the panel trapping us was now flipped up, teetering unsteadily on the back window. Glass shattered around the top with hazard lights sending unknown morse code blinks to the ceiling as the horn honked and an alarm whistled. Guess there's no hiding that we're out. The explosion we'd heard moments before was for the end garage stall, not the one closest to the home where we were.

Stepping into the garage caused the SUV, an Expedition, big, bulky and tall and yet I could hear the metal scraping then whining as it fell backwards. Wheels up, dead on arrival and sliding on the asphalt driveway, clearing a path for us. The pillar separating the middle stall of the garage and the one we were walking out of bent toward the far one, causing the garage door to buckle on the side until the wood snapped. Panels fell, dangling from the far side.

Each step I took with my friends behind me destroying a bit more of the home until we were in the driveway. A skirmish happening, with only Vince, those he considered his minions and me able to use our powers.

Riley stared, fish mouthed at me as I kept my hand out and those I was protecting behind me. Facing the home fully as I arced my way out of the garage. Vince's eyes, icy and angry, tried to bore into me. His focus having to shift from Riley, Trent and the others that had come with us to me. I could feel him. The power to block attempting to wrap around mine, to strangle the strength I possessed. My chest filled with pain, stabbing then pressure as if my heart was being crushed inside his fist. Vince was torn if the twitch of his eyebrow was any indication. Take on the pack or take on the one who was defying him.

Was my power as great as all of them combined? If I thought too hard about it, I might waiver. Instead, I focused, compartmentalizing any questions for later discussion. Now I had one goal, get the people out and one threat, Vince. Breathing slowed from pain more than necessity. Expanding my chest sent sparks of pain across my ribcage and down both of my legs. My right arm, extended weight a thousand pounds, causing pressure on my joints and my shoulder threatened to give way. I wanted to take in those behind me but feared breaking the lock I had on Vince would allow his hold on my heart to twist to the side. Plucking the organ and all my power from me.

His power was much like mine, an extension of himself. Mine came from my chest and while I held my hand out, I didn't need to in theory. I could be like Vince, whose power came from his mind. The sick and twisted part of him imagining ways to hurt others and extending those thoughts to his victims.

Others tried to attack. Fireballs slammed into my bubble, sending licks of heat across my face and down my back. My skin stung, but I didn't recoil. Wolves barked and ran toward me with a leap, only to yelp as they slammed into the shield and fell back licking injured paws. The impact tweaking my shoulder, but I stood steadfast. Backing away, Riley, Trent, Peyton and Summer slipping into my shield. I wasn't Riley. I didn't absorb their powers; their strength was another thing. In the field by the train, those I'd allowed into my protection were the burst of intensity for my shield. Knowing I was helping them, protecting them, keeping them safe. Not needing to see them but feeling their presence. Like when the air shifted upon a new arrival, you didn't need to turn to see them to know they were there.

When Imani entered my shield, the tentacles of Vince's power strangling my heart began to break off as if I were taking his fingers and bending them backward. Snapping the digit where it broke off from the hand. The sound reverberating and making Vince's lips twist in pain. Good. I wanted him in pain, the dislocated shoulder of Alex, the swollen eyes and caved in skulls of the others. The last thing Vince needed was a pass. And Taylor. Poor Taylor, who'd been so strong and defiant, now reduced to a compliant puppy afraid of her own shadow.

Deep inside, I wished there was a way for Taylor to get her revenge with Vince. Torture him, twist the knife into his gut because Imani said it was a painful way to die. But we would lose more of her with revenge. It wouldn't bring her back, no matter how satisfying it would be to watch.

Stepping forward sent Vince flying back into the same rock wall that had cut into my shins when I scaled the cliff's edge.

"Aren't you the tough one?" Vince said as he brushed off his shoulders and moved toward me. "Have you been practicing? How many little errors have you made? Aunt Judith's belly recovered from your last error."

My shield made a woo noise like a power drain, then recharged.

"Sensitive subject?" Vince challenged.

"She's been better since your mother arrived," I countered.

Vince broadened his chest. "Dear mother, she's still kicking around, well you know what they say?"

"No, tell me."

"A son's best friend is his mother." The dark scowl sending a shiver of doubt, much like I had when Imani had mentioned about Ms. Weston's past, allowed Vince to advance.

"Mommy issues aside," I rebuffed and stepped stupidly forward on my left foot. Instantly the pain shot up my leg, into my hipbone and my hand lowered enough Vince's eyes narrowed as if he saw an opening.

"You're strong and will be a nice addition to my army."

"Aggs," Riley said. "We have Taylor and the others, let's go."

"Yes, tuck tail and run," Vince said. "Too bad she's stronger than you and won't allow a push, even from one of her favorites."

That's what Vince wanted, a chance to regroup and give doubt to our ranks. Strength comes from hope and friendship. He only knew how to pull it from control and fear. That was fleeting and useless. Only as strong as the next news cycle at best, unless compounded.

Love was the same, only stronger.

"Is that Imani?" Vince asked with a lilt in his voice, as if seeing an old friend.

Doubts, seeds sprinkled like glitter, hard to get rid of no matter how many times you vacuum. Had Imani done this to me? Tested me? My loyalty when it came to Ms. Weston. See how we reacted and had I passed? Had I? Calling a council meeting?

"Shhhhh, Little One, silence those voices," Imani said.

"Are you with him?" I questioned, feeling myself weaken, the resolve, the belief coursing through my veins suddenly wavering. Much like my shield.

"You tell me," Imani said.

CHAPTER SIXTEEN

Security lights were ablaze around Vince's property, shadows lighting up the moonless night. Horns and sirens blaring and the only voice I heard was Imani. Vince's mouth was moving and there were mumbles behind me, but it was Imani. Asking me the question, an ultimate one about trust. Though he didn't touch me. He didn't wrap his arms around me and hold me. While I could feel his presence, I couldn't be distracted by the security his arms could bring me.

Unlike an abuser, one that coddles you, convincing you they would protect you. The danger you knew when they were violent was a mistake of your mind. No, Imani let me find my own truth. Didn't he say trust your feelings, the first instinct? Don't listen to the voices telling you who to trust, your body will tell you that. The natural instinct that causes a dog's haunches to rise with the uncle you never wanted to visit, while a complete stranger has them lowering their upper body and asking to play. Both approached the animal the same way, but there was something. The smell, the way they walked, or maybe animals could see auras.

Even now, I could count everyone inside my shield. I knew

187

who I'd pulled into my circle and who I wanted to protect. Without even seeing them, I knew they were there. Every soul touching mine on a plane invisible to the naked eye.

One Vince wanted to harness and twist for his own purposes, and one I refused to allow. Stepping forward once again, pulling my friends with me in my heart, if not physically, was enough to press Vince into the door of his home and caused the cornerstone to move. Gordon had strength. Was he the one doing this? Or was I?

Did it really matter? The home was loosening with each step. Sliding backward with Vince and a handful of his minions struggling to slip from my hold. A woman with dark eyes and an angry glare was at the corner of the house and extricated herself, popping around to the side then disappearing in the darkness. Finally freed from my shield, that had been pressing her into the home that was moving.

My arm outstretched as Vince pressed against my hold, reaching back behind him to open the door to his home. He fell backward as the door sprung open. Tumbling backward he crab walked until the minions that had been hiding inside lifted him by his arms to right him. Shaking them off, he stalked toward me only to not see the scared little girl I'd been before.

Vince's deepest secret had been revealed. His weakness exposed, and I was there to revel it in all.

"What is the matter?" I questioned, keeping my hand out, the international sign to stop, but my assurance my shield would stay in place. "Can't handle a little girl?"

"Oh, the things I'm going to do with you. Proper training that is all it will take," Vince said, then tried to sprinkle more doubt. "Ask Imani, he is such a good lapdog, he even fetches. Don't you?"

Imani didn't answer, but it wasn't guilt shifting auras around me. The air in my bubble spiked with rage. What pulled the house off its foundation was the power behind that rage. Centuries built up, revenge fantasies and more swirled invisible around the space.

My next step had Vince's hands extending on either side of him, the home moving a yard at least to be away from me. The second step, I gingerly placed the heel of my left foot on the ground and rolled forward to avoid the pain that would diminish my shield slightly. Water spirted from the edges, from snapped pipes and the wind was coming off the ocean below. Hitting the unstable building from the side. Or maybe it was me. Would nature reclaim the home built to be one with it? The next step had me at the first step to his door and Vince's eyes widened.

"You might as well be a *Harvey*, Vince. To me you are weak, struggling to have value."

"Well, Charity, you know all about that," he challenged using the slur Taylor had used against me when I first arrived.

Her anger and superiority complex fed by a man who knew his own weakness.

"And yet, you're the one with others ready to flee. While behind me is an Army."

"One I control," he said. "Or haven't you noticed? They aren't rushing to your aid. Riley already called for retreat."

"And yet, he's still here." Cocking my head to the side, any imposter syndrome I'd felt in the past was vanishing with each step I took.

"Sticks and stones may hurt you, but what do you think I have in this home?" Vince reached for a homemade spindle chair and broke off a leg, making sure to point the splintered end toward me. "I know how shields work, Agatha."

Running, joust style with the jagged end extended, he slammed into my shield, sending a nauseating wave through me. The gut check sharp and painful as I dropped to a knee, then flung my hand back up in hopes of restoring my shield in time.

My hand rising in the air, I was shaken in my crouched position as my shield tossed Vince against the window with enough force the home teetered with me balancing on the steps. Still attached, and the home more than half over the cliff, I let my shield go. Fear or panic. Either way the weight of those behind me vanished, the final nail in my coffin as I saw the sea through the windows.

Not in the distance. The horizon coming into focus. No, it was rushing to meet the home, curving inward toward the rocks below. Sending my body, gravity defying toward what had been the top of the doorway. Catching it with my hands kept me from falling closer to Vince.

Once again, time slowed, each tortuous microsecond rushing at me in agonizing detail. Vince's face twisting then accepting his fate. Eyes closing, arms out, as if he were martyring himself to the ocean and boulders below. Waiting for the shattering of glass like a rock being thrown in a pond newly frozen. Being pulled under the waves and drug out to sea, only to be thrown back ashore then back out. The driftwood lifestyle floating one moment, then smashing into harder, stronger objects.

It was hard to kill *aberrations*. Isn't that what the elders said? Hard, but not impossible. We were not in one of the voids, robbing us of our powers. We could bring them out, and yet my shield was exhausted. Missing or finally being cut off by Vince in his last evil act on earth. Lord knew my chest was tight and from the moment we went over the edge of the cliff my breath had been snatched from my lungs. Soon I wouldn't need it since the impact would have taken it, anyway. Was it worth it? My friends were all safe, one of the greatest threats gone, turning into sea foam for all eternity like the real Little Mermaid. My life for the whole train. A fair trade.

Transfixed, I watched as the home shattered below me. The sea unforgiving when hit from the wrong angle and high speed. Crashing as if a semi had taken out a picture window. Pieces flying upward, trying to escape their fate before a wave washed away from the bits only to be fought back by another, coming from nature and swallowing the foreign objects.

Vince and I couldn't have been more than twenty feet apart, but from the time he was pulled under the waves to the point when the front door slammed shut on my fingers still holding on to the jamb may have felt like hours instead of seconds.

When my arms pulled back from the smash on my fingers, they were instantly locked to my chest and the distance between me, and the spray expanded. While the angry sea spit at me, I was not pulled in, my death delayed as I flew backward in an acrobatic spin through the air. Oxygen rushed into my lungs, reminding me what I needed to live in a world I had given into leaving. Pointing my right foot and curling my left leg into my savior, no doubt or confusion in my mind for who came to my rescue. The embrace one I searched for in my darkest moments over the last few days. The aura entering my shield boosting my power the greatest.

"You never answered my question, Little One. I hate being left on a cliffhanger."

"That is such as bad pun, oh Ancient One," I replied as he gently landed in front of Summer, in front of the *healer* who practically bowled us both over as she wrapped her arms around me and Imani by default.

"What did I tell you?" she scolded. "You can't leave me. And you are not allowed to die." Pulling back to look at me, Summer made sure to hold my face in her hands and slipped the skull cap from my head to free my hair. "Do you know how many people had to hold me back when the house went over the edge?"

I wanted to boop her nose and say one, tease her even with the tears staining her cheeks, but my arms were locked by the vice that was Imani's arms. His nose nestled into my collar bone as his lips rested on the edge, body steady but breathing ragged.

"Oh, Ancient One," I said, only to receive a muffled response.

"No, not yet."

If nothing else, I wanted to have my hands released so I could cling to his forearms like before, but he refused to budge. Instead, we were a statue on what remained of the house on the cliff. Electrical sparks popping with water gurgling from the ground, and I saw Riley standing at the top of the stairs to the dungeon, eyes staring down the steps into the pit. Waiving over others to see those who remained. The few we left behind because they could not walk or worse were unconscious. At least I hoped it was just that they were unconscious.

"Careful, Old Man. People might think you like me," I said, and Imani responded with a light, but warm kiss to my collar bone, hidden from others by the angle of my head, before releasing me enough that I could attack Summer back.

Wrapping my arms around her, letting my friend recharge me. The way we should have been doing on the train but weren't allowed because of the separation.

"Not to be a bother, but my foot is broken, and the adrenaline is leaving my body quicker than I expected."

"Two more minutes, please," Summer asked, not letting go of me, not that I was in a rush either.

Pain be damned, I was safe for the moment and moments were what got us through the dark times. In the distance, those who had been hurt by Vince were huddled together, a shared experience bonding them in a sick and twisted way. A group I was glad I would never have to be part of because Vince was gone. The threat removed.

The beat up converted U-Haul we used for retrievals rolled up the driveway with Gil, one of our contiguous helpers, cutting headlights across the damage.

"Leave the kids alone for ten minutes and they blow up the house."

CHAPTER SEVENTEEN

"Wait, what happened?" Summer asked, rousing me from my nap, though my eyes were struggling to lift. "Why aren't there subtitles?"

"They annoy me because they are rarely right," Breonna replied. "Basically, that is the pastor, and they just discovered he not only has three kids in the country, but he practices a form of hoo-doo or voo-doo, it's different over in Nigeria."

"That explains the blood being thrown on him," Summer replied. "I need subtitles, or I'll just be annoying you for the whole show. You realize that right?"

While my head was resting on a pillow, that pillow rested across Summer's legs as she ran her fingers through my hair. Though foggy, I remember her healing my foot in the back of the truck, then I snuggled in, finally finding sleep in the overcrowded moving truck next to someone.

Summer's fingers were running through my hair, not finding any knots, and I wondered how long I was out that my snarls were gone. Her healing powers, subconscious at times because I know I should be sore from all I'd been through and yet I might as well be sleeping on a cloud. Maybe I was. Did I die? Did we all die? The satisfied smile on Vince's face searing into my thoughts and shot straight up, making Summer jump.

"Warn a girl, damn," she said.

"What's going on? What happened?" I asked.

"On the show?" Breonna groaned and I shook my head.

"You don't remember?" Summer asked and pulled her legs underneath her to kneel on my bed.

"Did I die?" I asked.

"You better not have," Breonna said. "But in the off chance you're a ghost, any chance you have snacks in your footlocker?"

"I ate the last of them to get me through the night," Imani's disembodied voice came from my floor.

Peering over the edge of my mattress, I saw him, laying on his side, with his head propped up and resting on his palm. A pillow placed under his elbow giving him the cushion he needed. For the first time, his coat was off him and he wore a crimson t-shirt that clung to his very adult body. The muscles straining against the fabric and the angle giving me the view of a slice of his hip.

"What? You didn't want me to starve, did you? I've been here for three days and these two barely feed me." His face hadn't changed. The scar, jagged and uneven, still in place, but I'm not sure I would have wanted it to be gone. Too much about Imani was perfection. Like a model I'd seen coming out of a pool a long time ago. No idea what was being sold in the ad because I couldn't look beyond the eyes. "You okay, Little One?"

I nodded, then turned to Summer. "Have I been asleep for three days?"

"Pretty much. I walked you a few times to the bathroom, but you must not remember."

Stretching out my legs and rolling my left ankle, I was fully intact. My toes no longer screamed in agony, and I could wiggle them.

"You barely ate and fell into a hiberfast like that." Imani snapped his finger.

"Maybe it's because every time I tried to sleep this last week someone was bugging me."

"Dear lord, now you know why I go into a dark cave and sleep for twenty to fifty years." Imani sat up and placed his hand on mine. "Glad to see you're awake, Little One, I'm going in search of pasta."

My stomach grumbled at the word and heat flared on my cheeks. "Any chance—"

"You know what sharing pasta means?" he said and placed a chaste kiss on my forehead.

Cupping his cheek when he pulled back, I ran my finger over the part of the scar that was on his upper lip. "Yeah. I remember."

"We don't know if Vince is really dead," Summer explained without me asking, sending a chill down my back and Imani gripped my hand in his, kissing my knuckles. "Or if the theory was just that. A theory."

"He wasn't found," I replied.

"Did you want to go down and look for him?" Summer asked. "Because none of us did. We were focused on saving the few who were left behind."

"We had to," I replied meekly, and Summer pressed her forehead to mine.

"Food, she needs food, or she'll pass out from exhaustion." Imani left and Breonna immediately turned off the TV that had been hung and hooked up with cable.

"Oh my God, he's gorgeous," Breonna said. "I only left to get him food and bring myself back to earth."

"What are you guys talking about?" I asked, testing my legs, but using the wall to balance me as I stood.

"He hasn't left your side," Summer said. "Devotion

overload. We never saw him leave the room. I'm pretty sure he only went to the bathroom when we took you out."

While weak, my legs hadn't fully given way as I stepped around the pallet made on the floor Imani must have been resting on.

"We told him we had you," Breonna said. "How hard is it to randomly check and make sure you were breathing? But he insisted he had nowhere to go."

"He loves you," Summer said as I dug through my pile of clothes to find a zip up hoodie. "Like loves you a million times, forever and ever. We're never going to die so let's see the world love."

Turning on my heel, I faced the two of them who were both leaning forward waiting for me to confirm their suspicions. As if Imani and I had openly declared our adoration for each other. Sure, he'd said he would take me away, but he couldn't be feeling the way I did. Then again, he was offering pasta.

"I tried to kiss him in the forest, and he rejected me," I admitted, though why, while I was in front of Breonna, I don't know. Roommate or not, it was embarrassing. "When I created that crater, it was because I was hurt."

"By rejected, what do you really mean?" Summer asked.

"There was more emotion in my hand when we practiced at my house as kids," I said, holding my hand with the thumb tucked behind my fingers and bringing it to my lips.

"Mama always said love yourself first and love yourself best the rest will come," Breonna said.

"Not funny," I replied, zipping up my hoodie when there was a light knock at my door. Since I was standing, I opened to see Sadie waiting in the hallway.

"You're up." She smiled. "I was worried I would wake you. When you got here, you seemed half dead."

"Helps when your best friend is a *healer*," I replied.

"I bet." Sadie rocked back on her heels a bit. "Summer saved me when I first arrived."

"What do you mean?" I asked. "You said that before, were you shot or something?"

"Aggs, you ever notice no one has glasses or braces in Satori?" Summer questioned and glanced between the two girls. "No cerebral palsy, everyone has all their limbs, no—"

"I was born Simon," Sadie replied stopping Summer from running down a laundry list of things she'd fixed. "I wish people could understand how *healers* show our truths."

"DNA hiccups at times, I just remove the hiccups."

"We better not let the secret out. I know plastic surgeons that would have her locked up," I said because beyond the fact Sadie was taller than an average woman, there wasn't a part of her I would think hadn't come factory standard.

"She was uncovering the real me," Sadie said. "Nothing more, nothing less, although the recovery time was considerably better."

"It only works when the person truly was born in the wrong body," Summer said. "At least that's the best way I can describe it."

"Okay, well, this has been a fun look in the past, but I wasn't hoping for more than going back a few days," Sadie said. "You borrowed my hairdryer, then the world went wonky."

"Right," I said, heading back to my open footlocker.

"The rescues have finally cleaned themselves enough, I guess," Sadie said. "The showers are now open for business for us regular folks again."

"Decontaminated too," Summer said as I passed the hairdryer to Sadie, who gave a nod then left.

"How is Taylor?" I asked, and Summer's eyes turned down.

"Riley is with her for now," she replied. "A few others, too, rotating in and out. He's there to heal whatever she does to herself. Cynthia too, though she's more soul than body healing."

"Imani said she healed him after—" my whole body shivered, and I wrapped my arms tight to my chest.

Outside the door, footsteps were rushing and Summer's phone went off.

"Shoes now," she ordered, and I slipped on a pair of sneakers.

"What's going on?" I asked as she practically drug me, my finger caught in the back of my shoe as I pulled in on having nasty flashbacks to the last time this happened and wanting to get her to stop. "Jesus, Riley two-point O let me walk."

"No, I need to hold your hand," she said.

My heart instantly dropped, and I stopped, my feet planted enough, she stumbled a bit as I clasped her hand hard.

"They didn't find him, did they?" I asked.

"Find who?"

"Vince?" I questioned

"No."

"What about Imani?" I asked, my heart tightening more.

"What about him?" she replied. "Come on."

"Is it true?" Gordon asked, running up to us. "Is it true?"

"Stop, he knows. I don't so at least tell me the rumor," I said. "Because I'm not moving otherwise."

People were emerging from their suites to see why people were running up and down the hallway. Not really down, no, everyone was going in the same direction, which meant we were going to Peyton's. Intel, info, something had the train on high alert.

"The results are in, and Trent's dad just conceded the presidency," Summer said, and I placed my free hand to the wall only to smoosh fresh blueberries.

"I was bringing you pasta, Little One. No reason to destroy the crops," Imani said, pulling my hand from the wall and using his jeans to wipe them clean. The smell of oregano and basil hanging in the now uneasy air. "Heard a rumor I'll be allowed to use a washing machine tomorrow. Might as well make the soap work, right? What am I missing?"

"In two months, Trent's dad won't be president," Summer said, giving my other hand a light tug. "You coming?"

"It never stops, does it? I got three days of sleep and now we're back in the muck."

"Muck? What muck?" Imani said, following as we stumbled our way toward Peyton's room.

"Every day a new plan. Do we ever get a break?"

"I do have a nice place, if you want to check out for a good decade or two," Imani offered.

"I want to live my life," I snapped. "I've lost high school, no prom, no graduation, no homecoming, no driver's ED."

"Slow down both of you Little Ones. It's a position, temporary at best," Imani said. "Even the first guy didn't want to put in more than eight years."

"The little bit of hiding we are currently afforded comes from the fact the president can control the transportation department. The railroads," Summer said emphatically, while her hand waved around the railcar.

Ms. Weston must have been tagged to come along for the planning process as I saw her disappear into Peyton's room, then reopen the door as we approached.

"Double portion," she said, eyeing the to-go containers Imani held in his hand.

"Pasta night," he replied, and she nodded.

A countdown clock was lit up on the wall in Peyton's room as the group piled inside. Trent came from around the partial wall with his phone in his hand. His face white as a sheet as Summer went to his side, wrapping her arm around his waist and brushing back the hair that had fallen in his face. The two of them speaking with their eyes, no words needed, the connection evident to everyone in the room.

On the big screen, the President-Elect walked out on stage in a large arena. Red, white and blue balloons dropping from the ceiling mixed with confetti as he waved. A smile plastered on his face with his wife, helmeted headed as good politician's wife should be.

"That is him, right?" Imani asked Ms. Weston, who's lips were pursed as she nodded. "Yeah, that's what I thought."

"Who?" I questioned the elders as the camera swooped through the crowd. Signs with the candidate's name, mixed in with hopes for the future and one that made us all pause. Or maybe it was Peyton pausing live TV so we knew the danger ahead.

Humans Only. The words simple, but when Peyton pressed play, we could all hear the commentator speaking about the pledges made on the campaign trail that won him the election. Least of which was finally rounding up those outliers that President Marcus had let slide. Sympathy coming from a man with his own homegrown mutation.

"Tell me you don't have a kid that's gifted, without telling me you have a kid that is gifted," Gordon said.

"He did," Imani said.

"What do you mean he did?" Peyton asked.

"His daughter, Lissa, the last *amalgam*."

"Wait!" I held my hand up to catch up. "Lissa, as in Vince's wife, which means the new president is an *elder*?"

"Yes," Ms. Weston said. "And that clock is useless. We need to be off the rails as soon as possible."

Slipping my hand in Imani's, I squeezed, leaned up against him, and closed my eyes.

"It'll be okay, Little One," he said. "We have a few months. And we'll be settled in and safe before my birthday."

"Let me guess, you are thinking about cake."

"Ugh, yes," Imani said, "But don't worry, I saw donuts."

"Did you now?" I replied, my head becoming light as he pulled a white paper bag with grease stains from a coat pocket. "I need to go lay back down."

Summer perked up, worry furrowing her brow.

"Her sugar is low, she needs food," Imani said. "Sorry about your dad, but honestly my hidey-hole can only keep a handful of us comfortably."

"We're not hiberfasting," Ms. Weston said. "But that man will be coming for us."

"You're going to have to go to him," Imani said, and Ms. Weston shook her head, pulling in on her lips. "This generation is different, the world is different. We know that and wherever he's hiding, he knows it too."

"Who?" I asked only to get a hushed response from Imani.

"Rodem."

"Peyton, I know you have ideas. Where are you thinking of hiding us?" Ms. Weston asked. "Just know, there's a chance we could end up with up to a hundred elders."

"That's optimistic," Imani said as he nodded toward the screen where our future president, Nathaniel Downing, was making his acceptance speech. "We know at least one that won't be joining us."

"No, he will be hunting, along with those who follow him."

Imani nudged me toward the door. Slipping away down the hall he led me to my room and let me settle in before passing me a container with spaghetti in it. We didn't speak as we walked. People called out questions as if I actually would know the answer. The silence continuing even when we got into the room. He fluffed pillows around me, and we sat next to each other in my bed. Breonna wasn't in the room, and as I nervously spun the noodles on my fork, I couldn't bring myself to bring it to my lips.

"None of that. I've given you love right there." Imani lifted my down-turned chin. "What is wrong with my Little One?"

There were many things I had little to no interest in knowing. The GDP of nations, where I'd be in five years, hell five months. I wasn't the one who wanted to plan, I only wanted to go along for the ride. Do my part, but not be in charge. That was for Summer or Dina or Claire. The Westons and Trent.

Knowing where I stood with people was something I wanted to know. No, needed to. When it came down to it I needed to know the trust I extended was also returned to me.

"Why didn't you kiss me back?" I asked, not sure the heaviness in my stomach was for the next disaster or the response I was about to get. Or where I found the boldness to even ask the question.

"In the forest?" he questioned.

"Was there another time I missed?" I asked.

"No, I was buying time," he confessed, his hand sliding from my knee to my inner thigh before he snapped it back. "Remember how I said Gordon looked familiar?"

"Yeah."

"You do too, but not like reincarnation in the exact same body and face, but you remind me of one I've lost," he said. "Judith and I have spoken of it before. Reincarnation, our souls coming back."

"Are we all—" I spun my hand, rotating at the wrist as if that would pull the word out of me.

"Shadowed? No, not even slightly. You, Gordon, Louise."

"Who's Louise?" I asked, and he lifted his head toward Breonna's bed. "Breonna."

"Breonna, right. I knew her as Louise, a blonde French girl from the country."

"We all exact opposites?" I question.

"Gordon looks like the Scotsmen I knew." Imani shook his

head. "To Judith, I'm a girl from the mountains. Must be why I don't hate flying or hights."

"Pigtails? Unwavering love for your grandfather, loved frolicking in the fields?"

"First off, Little One, every non sociopath loves a good frolic." He gave me a wink and the first smirk that didn't annoy me. "Secondly, not when she knew her. Before my time, obviously, and before Heidi. More of a Hessian assassin, covered in the blood of her enemies."

"I'm going with the girl with milkmaid braids."

"Geez, a guy dresses up once for a masked ball and he gets typecast," he said, then nudged me with his shoulder.

We sat in silence again, the fork heavy and me unwilling to bring it up until this was settled. "I was someone special in your life before?"

"There's a shadow on you. A shadow only those who've known you before see and only at the right angle. The thing is, much like with Gordon, you've come back, but are not the same."

"And this version of me you don't like?" I asked, bringing the fork to my lips. A bit of self-soothing with food, allowing me to lift the utensil finally.

"That's the thing. The shadow is there, but you are who you are. We've yet to determine if it is souls changing and shifting or simply their powers flowing into someone, but it doesn't mean at a base level I'm not naturally pulled to you. Once around you I see and feel the difference."

Did I need to repeat my statement?

"I wanted to make sure what I felt for you was for you, and not the shadow of who'd you been in the past."

"And now?" I asked, unsure I wanted to the answer.

Imani turned my head toward him. "I see you, Agatha. A girl on the verge of being a woman that I very much am enamored with."

This time he leaned in, his thumb sliding along my jaw as our lips touched. The scar uneven on the top lip, giving him depth and texture. When his lips moved to the side, my mouth opened slightly. Body warming to the gentle touch as his fingers ran through my hair, and he cradled the back of my head in his hands. A kiss, warm and soothing. One not forced and not rejected. When it broke, I didn't feel abandoned as his forehead pressed against mine and my eyes nearly crossed staring into his.

"Now eat, Little One," he said, giving me a gentle peck on my lips before leaning against my wall. "The next few months will be a blur and you will need fuel."

"Random question," I said, leaning my head on his shoulder as I slurped up a forkful of spaghetti.

"Plaid."

"Huh?" I questioned

"Random answer," he replied.

"You said we'll be settled in by your birthday," I said pushing the pasta around in the bowl.

"We better be, your protector loses power on January twentieth, right?"

"I guess," I replied, not knowing the exact date, but seeing as Imani had been around for a millennia he'd probably attended at least one inauguration.

"Then by the fifth of February all the pictures should be hung and electricity on and there better be a cake with buttercream frosting."

"February fifth," I clarified.

"Depending on the calendar, but since an *aberration* created the Gregorian calendar, that's the one we all tend to default to for our actual birth. Why?"

"No reason," I replied with a half-smile, wondering if what Taylor had been muttering might actually be true. "Just a rumor I'd heard."

Keep reading for a first look at book 3 in
The Aberration Series,
coming 2022 from
Fire & Ice Young Adult Books

Don't miss your next favorite book!
Join the Fire & Ice YA Books newsletter today!
www.fireandiceya.com/mail.html

THE SEER

THE ABERRATION #3

CHAPTER ONE

Knowing you're in a dream is far from believing you're in a dream. There's a fine line when it comes to nightmares, especially when you're in class and wide awake. Being a daydreamer had my parents coming to the office more times than either parent wanted to. Then again, coming to the office for anything beyond being told your child was earning a special reward would be more than any parent wanted to do. Now my mind was wondering if that actually happened. Probably not, that was note-worthy. A letter sent home to mom and dad with a child living in fear from the time the last bell rung until their parents had the letter it hand. Quite sadistic if you think about it.

Sadly, I was back in the office for daydreaming. More of the screaming when the soldiers came in, shot my teacher and held a gun to my head. Only there were no soldiers. We were reading from a comic book version of *Midsummer's Night Dream*. Just a few scenes, short enough to play out thirty minutes, I'd been assigned Puck for obvious reasons. The class clown, if it weren't for my perfect grades and the fact on the idiot tests, I graded above a high school graduate, both in reading and vocabulary, I would have been kicked out long ago.

Hard to be on an IEP, independent educational plan, when your grades say you probably would have no issue in classes four years ahead of where you were. Being already two years ahead, another four would put me in college and I'm not sure my mother could handle the lack of social media posting access.

"Mr. Lark," Principal Neuman called, his pot belly straining the bottom buttons of his shirt. Thankfully, the ridiculous tie he wore covered the poor things.

What may have been a joke when he'd been a teacher now became his trademark. The man had to own the largest collection of tacky ties in the Tri-State area. One would hope no one else would wear them with pride, daily, even to high-class functions. Today's tie appeared new and was some sort of fish. Bass, walleye, perch, who knew it wasn't something that interested me. While the ties were supposed to breakdown the barrier and bring the student or parent ease at the authority figure, having a dead fish eye looking up at me had the exact opposite effect.

"Cool tie," I said, not wanting to break with the tradition the kids had allowed me to join in with as I went into the cramped office and sat.

Being smart in high school is hard. Being taller than most of the teachers and students is harder yet. Being twelve, while being the former, in high school is the hardest.

"Your parents are on their way, but until they get here, how about we talk?" Mr. Neuman suggested.

Really? Without my parents? Now why would this man want me to do that? The last thing I wanted to do was speak to Nutty Neuman with his feel good, but gotta be tough mentality. This outburst should have been handled by one of the three vice principals if memory served. Then again, this was my fifth outburst in as many classes. Why my dreams couldn't stay locked away in my unconscious state I would never know. Then again, with how boring I found the classes, they may be in my unconscious.

Paying attention was key, watching as Mr. Neuman's mouth moved, and eyebrows raised. Trying not to get distracted by the white bits of gunk forming on the corners of his lips before he took a drink from his thermos. The smell of old coffee filled the air around me and I gripped the steel covered in faux leather armrest of my chair. I was drifting again, lost in the moment, and was teetering on the edge of another daydream. The frequency with which I'm being attacked by them had me reading up on schizophrenia and other mental disorders.

"We know you're bored in classes," Mr. Neuman stated, his tone enough to keep me from running down a rabbit hole. "That doesn't mean you can become a real Puck."

"What did you say to my son?" my mother snapped as she stepped into the office with my father in tow.

Practically stumbling from his chair, Mr. Neuman stood and held his hands at his waist but palms flat accidentally tipping over his thermos. The clattering of which as it rolled to the floor had my mind flashing to dream from first hour and I shook my head to clear it before it hit me with full force. Déjà vu, the plague of my existence, it seems as of late.

"Puck, he's playing that role in Ms. Gardner's class," Mr. Neuman bent over to get his thermos as my mother slid her hand over my shoulder protectively. "Did he not tell you?"

"Of course he did, we discuss Peyton's school work every night at supper," my father stated, jaw tight and frustration showing in his dark eyes. "Did Ms. Gardner misread the play?"

"No, no," Mr. Neuman indicated for my parents to sit in the last two seats in his office as he closed the door this time. "Nothing like that. I've been reviewing Peyton's record with the other administrators and this isn't his first outburst in class."

"Outburst? We weren't even told there was an issue with Peyton," my mother admonished, folding her peacoat and setting into the meeting. "Not even a letter home."

"We try our best to keep the parents out of our discipline—"

"Discipline," my father barked. Being a surgeon, I knew there was a high chance he'd pushed back a patient or worse yet, had a colleague covering call. "You've been disciplining our son without our knowledge."

Biting my lips, I fought the urge to jump up and whoop. No reason to encourage what would happen when I got home by being my father's champion now. While outwardly I could see they were on my side, internally I knew grounding was only level one of my punishments.

"Minor infractions," Mr. Neuman pleaded.

"That will be on his record, and we had no knowledge of it," my mother countered.

"Have you been pencil whipping our son?" my father asked. "I demand to see his record, the full one."

"No, no, I swear—"

"Don't, we want it now," my father said. "Peyton is a special child with potential beyond your imagining. Now I don't know if it's his brain, age or skin color that's intimidating to you, but you will not hamstring my son with little digs at his character. Especially with no indication to his parents who and why he is being chastised."

The back and forth lasted less than five minutes, with my mother and father winning the argument, but when I got home, I would be the casualty of the war.

"We could easily put him in one of the dozen private schools that offered him entry," my father said as he stood. "But the variety of classes here, and the fact his older siblings have matriculated from this public institution, gave us hope you could handle our son. Obviously. we were wrong."

"I've been speaking with the local middle school principals, and I reviewed Peyton's birthday."

"No, you don't," my father snapped, his finger cutting through the air like a switch cut from a tree. "My son is not one of those freaks."

"He fits the criteria," Mr. Neuman stated, and my mother stood, yanking my shirt to pull me up as well. "We don't know—"

"Exactly, we don't know, but last I checked, my son hadn't electrocuted anyone, started a fire with his bare hands or threw a car in a fit of anger." When my father crossed his arms, it was more than a barrier, it was a warning, one Mr. Neuman was as oblivious to as he was his ties' appeal.

"Peyton is almost thirteen, and we aren't sure what these abnormal—"

"You have no idea what you're talking about," my mother countered. "I'm insulted that you would put my child in with those freaks."

While I was allowed to be special, it was more of in a picture-perfect way when it came to my mother. The middle child of five, I learned early on, probably before I could lift my head on my own how to pose. What a camera was and what was expected of me when it was pulled out.

Social media wise, in public, we were the perfect family. Perfectly curated pictures, even the ones that were supposed to show how crazy we could be with tongues sticking out or tossing a cake in our face. At times, I wondered what was real and what was an image. To the world my mother was a volunteering supermom, with five kids, boy, girl, boy, girl, boy as if she'd planned it that way. Spaced as happy surprises, but I knew better. I'd been more than aware of the fertility struggles my parents had starting with me. But Sandra Lark had a brand. One, to me, my father indulged a bit too much.

"I want his full record printed out now and we will have a line-by-line discussion when I've reviewed it," my father warned. "What class are you missing?"

"Trig," I said meekly.

"Get back to class. I'm sure you can give him a pass to avoid another infraction on his record." The stare burned from my father and asserted on Mr. Neuman made me wonder if he was one of those laser beam kids. Lord knows Mr. Neuman moved fast enough to make one wonder.

Three days later, it wasn't my scream that was real. It belonged to others, and I had no reason to scream because what was playing out had tormented my waking and sleeping thoughts. I'd seen the movie and knew when to jump. Only they weren't soldiers, they were men who believed they'd been ordained by God to save the world from creatures like me. Ms. Gardner's head splatted on the white board in an arch as the bullets riddled her body. The drills on active shooters automatic only the shooter was in our room. We couldn't duck or cover, there was no blocking the doorway and piling desks until we heard the all clear from the police. The others in the class didn't need to fear, not that I could explain that to them. I knew the second gunman was for me.

The rest of the class scattered to the edges, and I stayed put, script in front of me and decided the time to lie was now if I ever was to survive. My acting was beyond sub-par, then again, I doubted this man was a Rhodes Scholar or a fan of the theatre, r-e version that at the least.

"You brought a gun." I shook my head and stood. The man flacked up with patches that has as much meaning in the world as my little sister's sticker collection. Sure, they were pretty, but in the grand scheme of things it meant we went to Disney one year and Wall Drug the next. For this weekend-warrior-wanna-be, my only hope came from my size and the fear of the unknown. "When you don't even know what power I possess, let me guess, you did a search for two-thousand babies with the county registry. Then cross-referenced with the schools and found out one wasn't in the middle school. Thought two of you would be enough to handle me while the rest of your monosyllabic knuckle dragging friends mowed down the middle schools."

Each step I took forward, he took one back, his hands trembling and finger nowhere near the trigger. My dream, while partially true, had been little more than a warning. One with no time, just a place for me to avoid. Only I couldn't avoid English class forever, no matter how much I wanted to. They would find me, kill my teacher as if Ms. Gardner would have some heroic gesture and try to save me. The thought alone ridiculous.

"What about these kids? They haven't determined if it's only us kids born in two thousand that got it." Another step while his friend tried to get him to focus, but his gun was swooping through the room now, as I wasn't the only threat to him or his automatic gun wielding friend.

"Don't throw us into this," Gunner, a kid who'd been held back a year said. "You know none of have that crap you freaks do. Don't listen to him, all he has is a big brain."

"One that's trying to control you, Roy, don't let him," his friend hollered, though I noticed the sweat practically draining down his face.

"Something tells me control is in your future," I replied, glancing over at Ms. Gardner, her eye fixed and open, the other side of her face gone. Lord knew where the other eye was.

Hunting the mutants or not, he'd killed a teacher. My teacher and while not my favorite, it still shouldn't be a job where you'd get killed outside of a random electrocution from a frayed wire the school didn't have the money to replace. But I lived in suburbia, and we had the money for the best of everything and none of the money was put into basic security.

"Tell me something," I asked, both men nearly jammed into the door frame. "Who truly has the power in this situation?"

Five years later

By seventeen I'd experienced more than my fair share of wet dreams. Honestly, I'd woken in piss-soaked sheets some mornings until early elementary, even with an early evening cut off for liquids. That was then replaced with the prepubescent dreams brought on by the funny feeling I got when I saw a pretty girl. My current soaked clothing wasn't the shameful urine, or the satisfaction of the hormone induced dream of a perfect girl. No, my back was soaked as if from a fever inducing dream. With a quick roll to sit on the side of my bed, a chill ran down my back, causing me to twitch. At some point, I should be allowed to outgrow rubber sheets. Really, it was a mattress cover made for liquid spills, but I was closer to being an adult than a child. Sadly, my sweat was far from a pop exploding when it opened wetting the sheets.

Running my hand over my normally clean-shaven head, I glanced at the outline of my body. The pale blue sheets darkened in a practical chalk outline type of way, and I knew they would have to be washed. My pillow too. Claire, my girlfriend, told me I never move until I wake up and thankfully, she was on the other side of the bed. I've stopped screaming most times. At least I learned to control my escape from the dream.

Sweating soaked my shirt completely and the top of my

shorts. Standing, I took off my t-shirt and tossed it on the floor. Blessed to have my own bathroom, I crossed to the small three-quarter bathroom. Running the water, the blessing it was slightly above freezing, gave me a chance to splash water on my face. The cold waking me fully from the nightmare currently plaguing me. At one time it had been distance. Now I walked freely, replaying options, and trying to force a different outcome.

Bracing on the pedestal sink, I stared at myself in the mirror. My head in desperate need of a shave, not my face so much, but my hair had grown in a bit, and I knew I would need to get rid of it. Growing up, I would go to the barber at least once a month. Getting lined up, even if my hair was long with thick curls, I kept the sides short.

A soft, familiar hand glided up the center of my back as a second came around my stomach and I captured that one with my own hand. Bringing the delicate hand to my lips and kissing the center of Claire's palm.

"Again," she said as she rested her cheek on my back. How she could stand it, I don't know. I needed a shower. I'm sure my skin was sticky if not wet still. "Same one, Peyton?"

"I better clean up," I said tapping her hand three times to signal her to release me, but she wouldn't. Not now, not after the dream that attacks at night. "Baby."

It was useless. Claire could see deep inside of me and wouldn't allow me to get a pass. One of the many reasons I cared for her, the love she showed me nearly three-fold.

"I checked the calendar," she said, and I closed my eyes, not wanting to hear what she would say next. My tracker, my other half, the one person I can never lie to and who sees the real me all the time. "Eight days. It's been eight days."

Eight days since this vision haunted me. The curse of being a *seer*. Visions came to me all day long. Some small, some big. All confusing the real from the imagined when they are vivid.

This one choked me, tangled me, pulled me under and I was spun. Only it was a repeat. Possibly giving me new information, but I didn't want to document the dream with the others in my notebook.

The stack high with college ruled sheets filled with convoluted dreams. Starting when I was young and had night terrors. My mother telling me to tell her the stories to get them out of my head. As if telling the nightmare would make it go away. She started writing them down when my nightmare came true. She told me to write my own. No knowledge, no guilt, I assume. Not sure why, school shootings, even at elementary schools, were sadly normal. What made her think I had some psychic power? I didn't. Psychics could focus on a person, I got visions. Some simple, some twisted.

Claire tried to get me to type them up and catalog them, but I had gotten too used to writing them down. Plus, the computer was my escape. The last thing I wanted to do was cross the world of make believe and reality. My visions did that enough for me.

"You know what it means, denying it only makes it worse," she said, sliding to my side.

Her tiny frame barely coming to my chest. Her normally silvery hair was an ash blonde, and I ran my fingers through it hoping it would ease her worry. Instead, it darkened more. *Soul readers* wore more than their heart on their sleeve. Every bit of her worry played out in her eyes and hair. Gorgeous when fire red, with eyes ruby. Sadly, her worry was dark. Never to the point of midnight, at least not in a few years. I'd been there when she arrived, dark, curled in a ball from and aching belly as she had been in my nightmares.

"I'll shower, regroup and try to process, that okay with you?" I questioned, not wanting to sound irritated even though I was.

"I'm going to get dressed and check out the fresh snow,"

she acquiesced, her hand trailing on mine. "I heard Gordan, and Petra finally have that greenhouse set up in the courtyard. Maybe I'll get you something."

I caught her hand in mine and pulled her back, capturing her lips for long enough, her hair deepened into an amber shade for a moment.

"It's fine, I promise," I said when I broke from the kiss. "Let me shower, check the world and meet you in the courtyard."

Watching as she pulled on pants and a sweater, before tying her hair back, I was hoping the red tint would stay, but the darkness fade away. Sadly, it didn't. At least her eyes were a shade of blue, that gave me hope as she tugged on a hat.

Flipping on the spray, I waited for it to warm up, knowing it may never get more than lukewarm. At least I have a space to think. Doubled up only because Claire and I were a couple, not out of necessity. The latest hiding place in disrepair we got for a steal under the shell companies and cash given from the elders. A former asylum, tucked away on an overgrown island in the middle of a lake, currently iced in since we had moved into Canada. Crossing through a mix of leaping, cash payouts and weak spots in the border. Countries no longer mattered to us, those born in the year two thousand. The *aberrations* were a country unto themselves, for the time being.

That time slowly slipping away, this time the soldiers would be real and would win. I hadn't been able to find a way out of it. The twisted dreams now compounding the main one had us regulated. In locked dorms or prisons. At first, I thought it was the asylum we found. The rooms have heavy metal doors that could be locked from the outside. A feature we quickly remedied before taking up residence. Too many in Satori, the country we'd created, had been in camps before. Government run, easily identified by the smiling faces on the brochures and the screams of pain on the inside.

No, move in day wasn't enough to stop the dreams which meant all in Satori were going to be taken. At some point, a government from some country would capture us, lock us away and this time there would be no escape. I'd game them all as if I were playing a video game, waking before losing all my lives and still I hadn't figured a way out. In less than a year we would be wearing matching uniforms and training for a war we didn't start or ask for.

Stepping in the spray my body seized the water mixing with the cool air hitting me in all the wrong ways. Why couldn't it have been a sex dream? At least then the cold water would have served a purpose. Instead, it was going to fill my lungs with pneumonia as I scrubbed off the sweat and tried to clear my head. There wasn't a cheat code to my dreams, God knows I've tried to find one. They had to be pieced together, I had to examine every nook and cranny to discover the out, but I was only one person and with no one able to meld into my dream I was on my own.

What irritated me the most was I was the sole person tasked with this cure. The *seer*. The one who is more accurate than a horoscope. All of it bull, because no matter how much I wander in a dream state I couldn't make this one stop.

Getting out I toweled off and headed toward the window of my room that overlooked the courtyard while I dressed. Corner room, top floor, for some a penthouse, for me a prison. Much like in the past I have a room of computers running twenty-four seven. Tapped into satellites and more. I watched as Claire cut through the thickening snow and into the new greenhouse. Fogged glass from the heat meeting the cold air housing the newly grown garden. There was little left of the courtyard itself. The squared space now had an arched building with dark figures moving inside.

A pain shot through my eye and into my skull, sending me stumbling backward and onto my bed. The vision crystal clear in my right eye while the left stayed locked closed, I no longer had the ability to fight it. Flipping on my stomach, my knees crashed into the floor, my upper body stayed on the bed as my head swum.

These were the worst visions, precise, in full high-definition glory and they could send me into a vomiting fit if I didn't get it under control. Slamming my right eye shut I braced, hands gripping the sheet ready for the ride.

A ride, with soldiers, electronic neck collars and a crumbling building. One that was very familiar and not in previous nightmares. Once again, our thoughts of safety trashed. There was no escaping fate, and that bitch was beating down our front door.

ABOUT THE AUTHOR

Michel Prince is a USA Today best-selling author who graduated with a bachelor degree in History and Political Science. Michel writes young adult and adult paranormal romance as well as contemporary romance.

With characters yelling "It's my turn, damn it!!!" She tries to explain to them that alas, she can only type a hundred and twenty words a minute and they will have wait their turn. She knows eventually they find their way out of her head and to her fingertips and she looks forward to sharing them with you.

When Michel can suppress the voices in her head she can be found at a scouting event or cheering for her son in a variety of sports. She would like to thank her family for always being in her corner, and especially her husband for supporting her every dream and never letting her give up.

Michel has been awarded Elite Status with Rebel Ink Press in 2013, the service award for her local RWA chapter Midwest Fiction Writers in 2013 and 2014, won Sweetest Romance at IREA and is a PAN member of RWA. She lives in the Twin Cities with her husband, son, and dogs, Bolt and Sawyer.

www.michelprincebooks.com

ALSO BY MICHEL PRINCE

YOUNG ADULT NOVELS WITH FIRE & ICE YOUNG ADULT BOOKS

The Aberration Series

The Amalgam

The Shield

The Seer (coming 2022!)

ADULT ROMANCE NOVELS WITH SATIN ROMANCE

The Growing Strong Series

The Guardian's Heart

The Queen's Heart

The Politician's Heart

The Teacher's Heart

Novels

The Rotation